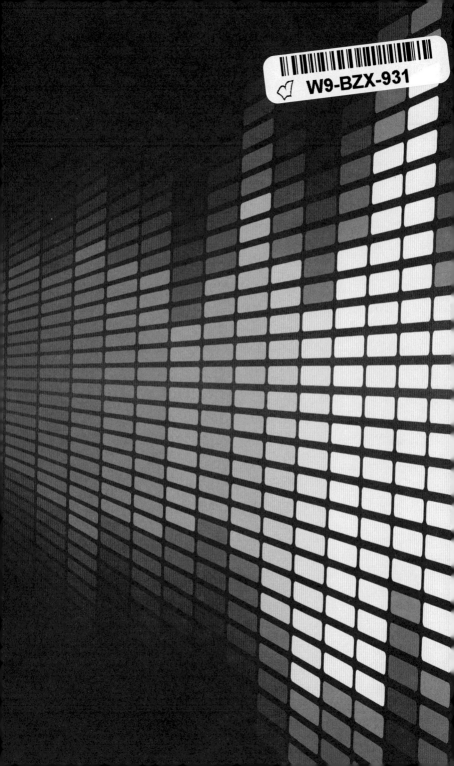

# BOYS LIKE YOU

## JULIANA STONE

# BOYS LIKE YOU

## JULIANA STONE

sourcebooks
fire

Published by Sourcebooks Fire, an imprint of Sourcebooks, Inc.
P.O. Box 4410, Naperville, Illinois 60567-4410
(630) 961-3900
Fax: (630) 961-2168
www.sourcebooks.com

Library of Congress Cataloging-in-Publication data is on file with the publisher.

Printed and bound in the United States of America.
WOZ 10 9 8 7 6 5 4 3 2 1

This book is for my daughter, Kristen. A young woman with a mind of her own and a love of books that runs in the family. I hope you never change.

# Chapter One

# Monroe

My gram told me once when I was eleven that I could do anything. She'd been very matter of fact as she poured us each an iced tea on a steamy afternoon.

It was the kind of afternoon when the air sizzled and stuck to the insides of your clothes. The kind of afternoon that made your skin clammy and your muscles lazy. I remember that the birds were quiet but the locusts chimed like mini buzz saws.

Funny, the things that you remember, and the things that you can't forget no matter how hard you try.

On that particular afternoon, we'd sat on her front porch in the rain, Gram's hyacinths bent over from the weight of the water, her two cats Mimi and Roger curled at our feet. I'm sure I wore some trendy New York outfit that was totally inappropriate for Louisiana in August, and Gram Blackwell was dressed in what she liked to call "genteel southern attire," which basically meant cotton instead of linen or silk.

We settled back in our chairs and chatted about the soccer

team. I told her how much I wanted to make first string, and she told me that anything was possible as long as I applied myself. Of course I believed her with all the enthusiasm an eleven-year-old who has never been hurt or disappointed feels.

Why wouldn't I? This was Gram, and she was never wrong.

I tried my hardest and made the team.

But that was before Malcolm. Before the awful year that had just passed. That was before I learned that my charmed life could bleed. That pain could become an everyday kind of thing, and that happiness was just a word that didn't mean anything.

And now, at the ripe old age of sixteen and a half, I don't know what I believe in anymore, and I don't know if I'll ever be fixed.

It's not like I haven't tried.

I went to private therapy. I went to group counseling. I read the books that I was supposed to read, did the relaxation exercises that I thought were stupid, and took the meds that they gave me.

In fact, I loved how those little blue pills made me feel nothing—which isn't very different from the way I feel most of the time—but medicated nothing is so much better than the real, hard nothing I had been living with.

I suppose it's why they weaned me off them. "Addict" wasn't exactly a label my mom wanted to add to the impressive list of everything else that was wrong with me.

My point is…I did it all. I tried.

It's just hard to succeed at something when you don't really care, and as much as I want to get better for my parents, I can't *make* myself care. Not even for them. My therapist says I need to care for myself first.

And therein lies the problem. The catch-22. I just don't care anymore. Not really.

Yet there are moments where, if I try real hard, I can close my eyes and smell the rain. Not just any rain, mind you, but *that* rain. From that long-ago afternoon.

Gram's rain.

"Monroe, I'm heading to town in a few minutes. Do you want to come along?"

I turned as Gram walked into the kitchen. It was nearly noon and I had been sitting at the table for about an hour, trying to decide if I was going to eat the bowl of pears she'd put out for me earlier or if I was going to put them back in the fridge.

I liked pears. I liked them a lot. I just wasn't all that hungry.

"Uh, I think I'll stick around here, if that's okay with you."

Gram put her purse on the table, and I pretended not to notice how her eyes lingered on my hair. I'd pulled it back in a ponytail yesterday—or maybe it was the day before—because I couldn't be bothered with it. I'm pretty sure I hadn't brushed it since.

She pointed to the bowl in front of me and raised her eyebrows, waiting half a second before grabbing it and setting it on the counter. She pulled plastic wrap from the drawer and covered the pears before putting them back in the fridge.

Gram turned and leaned against the counter, and for a moment, we stared at each other in silence.

I'd arrived a week earlier and we hadn't had a real chat yet—the one that I sensed was coming—and my stomach churned at the thought.

Gram's long hair was swept up in a clip at the back of her head, the silver strands glistening in the sunlight that poured in from the window above the sink. She wore pink lipstick, a casual cream skirt—cut to an inch above her knee—a moss-green blouse, and low open-toe heels to finish off the outfit. Pearls were in her ears, and the matching pendant lay at her neck. A classy choice that was totally Gram.

She was beautiful.

My gram had turned sixty last year and still carried that simple elegance that set her apart from a lot of women. She'd been a real hottie in her day, and though my mother said I was her spitting image, I didn't see it. But then I suppose beauty is more about your state of mind, and since mine was all dark and gloomy, that's what I saw when I looked in the mirror.

"All right," she said after a while and glanced at the clock above the stove. "I have someone coming by the house anyway, and I'll need you to show him where the job is."

Great. I thought of my bed and the nap I'd planned.

"Who is it?"

I didn't really care, but I could at least be polite and ask.

"I've engaged the services of a local contractor for some repairs and maintenance around the plantation. Today the fence around the family crypt and burial plot will be painted."

Gram's ancestors had lived in Louisiana for generations and this place—Oak Run Plantation—had been in the family for just as long. Years ago, Gram's father had turned the family home into a successful bed and breakfast/museum, which Gram had inherited, because according to my father, Gram's brother, Uncle Jack, was a no-good drunk who couldn't find his own butt if he needed to.

My grandmother even stayed on after her husband died, but instead of living in the big house, she moved into what used to be the carriage house. And that's where I'm staying this summer.

Everyone—which would be my parents and my best friend Kate—was hoping the hot Louisiana summer and laid-back atmosphere would somehow fix me. They think that the city and the memories are too much, and I don't have the heart to tell them that the memories will never leave. That much I've learned.

So location doesn't really matter, but I was glad to be away from my mother and her large, expressive, puppy-dog eyes. She looks at me a lot when she thinks I won't notice, and every time she does, I feel like the biggest failure on the planet.

I don't know how to react to her anymore—do I pretend I'm better to make her pain go away? Do I ignore her? Do I tell her to get out of my face?

And my father, God, he's the total opposite. He acts as if everything is normal. As if the last year and a half never happened—as if each one of us is whole—and that makes me angry. And kinda sad.

Gram grabbed her purse, bent low, and gave me a hug. "I love you, Monroe."

"I know," I whispered.

She grabbed her keys and paused. "Barbecue sound good for supper?"

I shrugged. "Sure."

"All right then." She moved toward the door but paused, her hand on the ivory handle. "He'll be here in an hour. Why don't you brush your hair?"

"Okay," I answered, though I'm pretty sure we both knew it wasn't likely to happen.

# Chapter Two
## Nathan

The crap thing about not being able to drive is that I do a lot of waiting around for rides, and I hate waiting. Doing nothing makes me crazy, and crazy Nathan isn't exactly the kind of thing I'm going for these days.

But mostly I hate waiting because it gives me too much time to think about the reasons I'm waiting in the first place. About how one stupid mistake changed everything. About how I screwed up so badly that now, the summer before my senior year—the one that I should have spent hanging with Rachel and Trevor and the rest of the guys—is going to suck.

Though it won't suck as much as Trevor's.

I wiped sweat from my brow and scooped up my bag from the porch. I hate waiting. I hate thinking.

In the fourth grade, Alex Kingsley tripped Trevor in the hallway, just outside our classroom. We had been in line waiting to head into the gymnasium, and Trevor tumbled into me. Long story short, we both wiped out, and the entire row of girls laughed their butts off. So did Alex—until we cornered him in the schoolyard at lunch.

Trevor and I taught the little turd exactly what happened to dickheads. After that, Alex pretty much left everyone alone, and though Trevor and I were punished—we had to stay after school every day for an entire week—it solidified our friendship.

We bonded over our mutual dislike of Alex Kingsley and our love of music and sports. Eventually, I forgave Trevor his thirst for all things country—he couldn't help it, his parents were true hicks—and he learned to like my progressive ear. He was into country music, bluegrass twang, and he also had a soft spot for the New York Jets. I was all about the old classics my dad loved, hard rock, and loud guitars. I also preferred the Dallas Cowboys, but he was cool with that.

Somehow we gelled, and our band is, or rather *was,* the hottest act in the area.

One mistake. One stupid-ass mistake and I ruined his life.

I would switch places with him in an instant if I could. Maybe then the guilt would go away. Maybe then I could look in the mirror and that empty hole in my gut would fill up with something other than loathing.

It should have been my future in the gutter. But I was Jack and Linda Everets's son, and around these parts, that meant something. Around these parts, it meant special treatment or a second chance, even when you didn't deserve it.

I'd gotten off easy and I knew it. Everybody knew it, except they used all kinds of excuses to cover up the fact that Trevor was lying in a hospital bed and I should be locked up.

*Nathan is a good boy.*

*He's never done anything like that before.*

*They can't be perfect all the time.*

*They all make mistakes, even the good ones.*

Blah. Blah. Blah.

None of it changed the fact that I'd screwed up huge, and I wasn't sure what made me more bitter—the fact that I should be riding a bench in juvie and wasn't, or the fact that I should be the one lying unconscious in a hospital bed with broken bones that would never play a guitar and a brain that might be scrambled for life.

My cell buzzed and I grabbed it from my pocket, frowning when I saw my uncle's name pop up.

Shit. I knew what this meant.

I started walking.

"Nathan, I'm going to be late."

The Oak Run Plantation was about thirty minutes down the road, and though the air was thick with humidity, anything was better than sitting on my front porch, staring at a car I couldn't drive and thinking about stuff that made me more depressed than I already was.

"I'll head over," I answered.

"It's hot as hell out there, boy. I don't want you to have heat-stroke. Your mother will tan my hide if that happens."

My parents had gone north for the week in a bid to escape the heat, so at the moment, I was stuck home with no wheels and no one to take me anywhere. I could die of heatstroke and they wouldn't know until Sunday night when they returned, because they never called when they were away—and I knew not to call them unless the house was on fire.

I could say it was because cell reception was bad, but the simple truth was, my parents really dug each other—still—and they kinda forgot about the world when they went away.

I used to think it was gross—the way my dad would paw my mom—but now I realize they have something special, and that's a hell of a lot more than I could say for a lot of my friends' folks.

"I'm good." I grabbed a bottle of water from my bag and emptied it over my head. It soaked through my hair, which hung down to just above my shoulders, and splattered drops of water across my white T-shirt. My dad hated my hair, but Mom and my girlfriend, Rachel, loved it.

Rachel had told me once that if I ever cut it off, she'd dump me—she was joking, of course, but for a while there I wasn't so sure.

It was hair; I didn't see what the big deal was, but Rachel thought it made me look like some guy on TV, and Rachel was, if anything, all about looks. I guess when you are a hot little blonde, it's not surprising.

"Thanks, Nate. You're a good kid."

*Tell that to Trevor,* I thought.

"The paint and brushes are already there, so you just need to get started and knock off around five, or earlier if need be. It's Friday, you got plans?"

Rachel had left for the lake about an hour ago with a group of friends we hung out with, including one of the guys in my band, Link.

I could still taste her cherry gloss in my mouth. She'd come by, wearing the skimpiest bikini top you can imagine, along with the shortest jean shorts she owned. If I cared enough, I would have given her crap about it, but since I didn't anymore, I said nothing.

She'd jumped from the car and into my arms, wrapped her legs around my waist, begging me to reconsider and come with them. She seemed almost desperate—as if she knew something that I didn't.

*What does it matter if you blow off Mrs. Blackwell?*

*Your job will still be waiting for you on Monday.*

*It's not like your uncle will fire you.*

"Nate," she'd breathed against my mouth. "Come on, baby, it will be a good time."

A good time for Rachel was code for getting wasted and having sex, which were two things I wasn't all that interested in anymore. At least not with her. Not since that night.

"Nathan?" My uncle's voice cracked through the cell.

"Nah, I'm taking it easy tonight. I'll work 'til five," I answered and then pocketed my cell. Or later. There was nothing for me to come home to, and without the band or Rachel around, what was there for me to do?

The walk to Oak Run Plantation was brutal. It was hot and muggy, and by the time I got there, my T-shirt was long gone. My feet were just as sweaty as the rest of me, and I was irritated that I'd decided to wear work boots instead of something more sensible like my Chucks or sandals.

The driveway was impressive if you were interested in that sort of thing, lined on each side by huge oak trees that were generations old. Their branches spread over the top, reaching for the other side like a canopy, and I enjoyed the shade as I walked toward the main house.

Several cars were parked beside a small outbuilding to the right, and at the last minute, I paused, because I was pretty sure Mrs. Blackwell didn't live in the main house anymore. I spied a smaller place on the other side, set back a good twenty feet. There were flowers planted in the front, beneath the veranda. Purple and white petunias just like at my grandparents. Old lady flowers.

I decided to start there first.

I dropped my bag on the bottom step, took the stairs two at a time, and rang the doorbell. A few minutes passed and I rang it again, this time pressing hard for several seconds. I could hear it echoing inside and took a step back.

"Shit," I muttered, glaring at the door—like that was going

to make it open. I was hot, sweaty, and didn't exactly feel like searching a freaking plantation for some creepy burial site.

One more minute ticked by before I decided that's just what I was going to have to do, when I heard a scuffling noise and the door swung open.

I'd just tied a bandana around my head to keep my hair out of my eyes, and with a smile plastered to my face, I turned back to greet Mrs. Blackwell.

Only it wasn't Mrs. Blackwell who stepped out onto the porch.

It was a girl. I knew that much. How old was she? I couldn't say exactly, because in that moment, I couldn't even tell you if she was pretty or not.

I was way too focused on a pair of eyes that hit me in the chest like a hammer against stone. The color was unusual—a light gray/green—and sure, they were pretty damn striking, exotic even, but it wasn't the color or shape that got to me.

It was what I saw inside them. Something indefinable and yet so familiar because it was like looking in the mirror, and my first thought as I stared back at her, my smile slowly fading away?

Man, that sucks.

# Chapter Three

# Monroe

The boy who stood on the porch was sweaty and half naked and not the old guy I was expecting. At all.

I suppose he was going for some kind of badass look with a red bandana wrapped around his head and his jean shorts hanging so low off his hips I could see the top of his boxers, but seriously?

Did all guys think us girls really gave a crap what brand of boxers they wore? Personally, I thought the whole look was ridiculous and couldn't imagine what it felt like to walk around with your pants falling off. Uncomfortable maybe. Ridiculous for sure.

He wasn't wearing a shirt either, and I'm sure that's why my eyes automatically focused on his tattoo. It was interesting to look at—exotic symbols in black ink—starting from the top of his shoulder and traveling down to just above his bicep.

I had never wanted a tattoo, but the summer before my world went into the toilet, I'd wanted a belly ring. Badly. All the girls at school were getting them, and I didn't think they came close to tattoos on the trashy scale, maybe a seven out of ten, but my mother was horrified at the idea. Her comeback had been, "that's something you can think about when you're old enough to vote."

End of story, because my dad is a wuss and always sided with her.

"Hey," he said.

I didn't answer at first and moved so I could peek around him, but there was no old guy, and he seemed to be alone.

"Are you here for the fence?"

His eyes narrowed slightly, most likely because I came off sounding rude. But in my defense, he was late and had interrupted my nap. And these days, napping was a pretty important part of my day. Too important, according to my parents, which was one of the reasons they'd sent me to Gram's for the summer. In the city, they were at work and I was alone—free to sleep as long as I wanted to and free to spend my days in pajamas.

Gram didn't let me hang in my pajamas. She might not have figured out how to make me brush my hair every day, but she sure knew how to guilt me out of my pajamas.

"Who are you?" he asked instead of answering my question.

"Who are you?" I shot back.

"I asked first."

*Okay, what are we, like, five?*

He scrubbed at his chin and sort of sighed. I got the impression that he wasn't exactly in a great mood, but then I wasn't either, so I guess we were even on that count.

I'm not sure how long we stood there, staring at each other with only the buzzing of the bees in the honeysuckle to fill the space between us. I shifted my weight, suddenly aware that my hair hung down the back of my neck like a limp rag. A limp, tangled rag that hadn't been brushed in days.

"Monroe," I finally answered.

"Monroe," he repeated, as if he didn't believe me.

I tugged my cami strap back into place.

"You have a problem with my name?"

He shook his head, "nope," and ran his hand across the back of his neck. I'm sure he did it because it pushed his chest out.

Pushed his chest out and emphasized his abs. Not that I was looking or anything, but it was kinda hard not to notice when he was so…naked.

"I'm just here to do a job." He stood back. "Do you know where the family bones are buried or not?"

I considered lying, but what was the point? Gram wouldn't be impressed, besides, it's not like I had to stay out there and keep him company. The sooner I showed him where the crypt was, the sooner I could get back to the important business of having a nap.

"Follow me."

I pushed past him and waited for the door to slam shut behind me before heading down the front steps and out to the back of the house. His supplies were set on the back porch, and I waited for him to grab them—a paint can and a couple of brushes—before following the stone path that led into the fancy gardens.

Gram's plantation is one of the fanciest in Louisiana. A Greek revival, it's been used in movies a few times, and while I don't find the house all that impressive—it's old— I've always loved the gardens. There is a maze to the left of the house, one I used to spend a lot of time in when I was younger, playing pretend or reading a book. And beyond it, set back on a small hill surrounded by mature oak trees, is the family crypt. It doesn't look as though it's far from the house, and I suppose it isn't, but by the time we reached it, I was breathing heavy.

Which was embarrassing, because I'm Soccer Girl—I'm in good shape—or at least I used to be back before I started taking naps every afternoon and not caring.

I turned and felt my cheeks flush when I found his eyes already on me. After clearing my throat and attempting to sound as normal as I could, I spoke. "What's your name?"

"Nathan," he said.

"Does Nathan have a last name?" Crap. Now he was going to think that I actually cared.

A hint of a grin touched the corner of his mouth, and God help me, but my cheeks stung even more. I bet they were as red as the apples in the bowl on Gram's table.

"Last name is Everets, and you?"

"Blackwell."

He tossed his brushes on top of the paint can at his feet. "Where are you from, Monroe Blackwell?"

Nathan approached the iron fence, which was faded and chipped and looked like a black and white cow had exploded all over it.

I shoved my hands into my back pocket and blew a curl out of my eye.

"New York."

"And you're here because…"

*I'm here because no one knows what to do with me.*

"Look, I don't really want to do this talking buddy thing, so I'm just going to let you get started, okay?"

He shrugged but didn't say anything, and for some reason that irritated me. I wasn't used to being dismissed like that. I was used to being under a microscope—used to having every action analyzed and picked apart. I was used to my parents, teachers, and friends hanging onto every word that came out of my mouth as if it was gospel.

Of course, the gospel according to Monroe isn't exactly full of rainbows and unicorns, but as long as I was talking, they were happy. Because a talking Monroe wasn't as scary to deal with as the nonverbal version I'd been several months ago. Back then, I was almost straitjacket material.

Back then…I shuddered. Nope. Not going there today.

Once more, I yanked on my cami straps, pulling on the material a little so that it wasn't plastered to my chest. Even though there was shade from the oak trees, I thought that it would be pretty awful to spend the afternoon out here painting. Because it wasn't just hot, it was oppressive.

It made me wonder about Nathan.

His shorts were Abercrombie, his boots Doc's—his aforementioned boxers, again Abercrombie. He didn't talk like an idiot even though the bandana was hick, and he looked like he came from money. It made me wonder why he was stuck out here painting some old lady's iron fence on an afternoon meant for pools or beaches. Or anyplace other than here.

He glanced back at me, and I turned quickly, because even though it looked like I was staring at him—I wasn't. Well, I wasn't staring at *him* exactly.

"What does your tattoo mean?" I said in a rush.

"I thought you didn't want to talk."

"I don't," I stammered, hating how flustered I felt.

He didn't say anything for a moment; in fact, several moments passed before he looked at his shoulder and shrugged. "It's Celtic."

Wow. Wasn't he just brimming with information?

"Celtic, as in…"

He cleared his throat in that way my dad does when my mom grills him about something and he doesn't want to answer. For whatever reason, this Nathan was more closed off and unfriendly than I was, which made me even more interested in him—or rather, in why he was like that.

"As in I don't know what it means, I just thought it looked cool."

I didn't believe him. You don't get ink for no reason.

"Well, at least you didn't get your girlfriend's name on your skin because…"

His head snapped up.

*I did not just say that.*

God. Now he was going to think that I was fishing to see if he had a girlfriend, and I wasn't. My cheeks stung and I knew they were even more red than before. Well, crap. Now he was really going to think I was into him, *in that way*.

Instead, he looked at me as if I was a retard. "That would be stupid."

Okay, so the girlfriend thing was a sore subject, and he totally didn't care what I was thinking. In fact, he seemed kinda pissed. "It's been known to happen," I retorted.

His eyes narrowed as if he was trying to figure me out, and that's when I realized it was time to go. I was sinking out here, and suddenly the effort to stay on solid ground was too much. I felt a little woozy and thought of my bed.

I took a step back. "Okay, I'll leave you to it."

"Sure. Nice meeting you, princess."

"It's Monroe," I shot back with the voice of a five-year-old. Hello. What was it about this boy that turned me into an imma-ture child with no filters?

Nathan bent over to open up his paint can without saying another word, and I hurried back to the house. Not once did I look back. Not even when I reached the maze and could have snuck a peek without him seeing.

I marched straight into the house and, once inside, drank two glasses of water before the weariness of my life—my very existence—pulled me down. It took way too much energy to be anything other than apathetic.

It was a heavy feeling and one I was used to, so I did what I always did when it hit. I trudged upstairs, flopped onto my bed, and thought longingly of the little blue pills that were no longer mine to enjoy.

I closed my eyes, turned and snuggled into my pillow, and prayed for sleep.

# Chapter Four
## Nathan

When my cell dinged for the fifth time in just over an hour, I swore and yanked it out of my shorts.

*Rachel.*

Did the girl not understand that some of us have to work? Didn't she know that some of us have court-appointed work dates to keep our asses out of juvie? Anger rushed through me with a hot, hard thrust, and I had to take a minute. What part of that didn't she get?

Ever since the accident, she acted as if nothing had changed. Like we were the same. Like she *needed* us to be the same to deal with the fact that Trevor was in the hospital and probably never coming out.

But I couldn't do that, and whenever I tried to talk to her about it, she shut me down. She tried to change the subject or tried to have sex. She was willing to do pretty much anything *not* to talk about that night, but pretending that everything was going to be okay was freaking exhausting.

God, Rachel was so exhausting.

I heaved a sigh and glanced at the text message.

Find a way to come. I miss u.

Her words were like sugar, but they made me angrier than I already was, and I considered calling her right there and then. I considered having it out *right there and then*, but after a few moments, I turned off my cell instead and shoved it into my front pocket. This had to be done face-to-face.

I dunked the edge of my paintbrush in the can and spread another coat of fresh black paint over the iron fence section I was working on. It was close to five and I was about half done with the job. I figured if I got an early start on Monday, I'd have the entire fence finished by noon. Or I could just keep painting until dark, because it's not like I had anything better to do.

I paused for a bit and grabbed a bottle of water out of my bag, my gaze focused on the smaller house, beyond the plantation home. I took a good long drink, not taking my eyes from the place.

Monroe.

No, more like Princess Monroe. I smiled at that. Princess Monroe with the big chip on her shoulder.

What the hell was her story?

I suppose most guys would consider her hot. Heck, I considered her hot. That little tank top she had been wearing showed some curves, and with all that dark hair and big eyes, she was definitely nice to look at. But her attitude was not something I wanted to tangle with. I was pretty sure she was high maintenance and a snob to boot. She was from New York City, after all.

Shit. I screwed the cap back onto my water bottle and tossed it back into my bag. Technically, I was still with Rachel, even if mentally I'd left weeks ago, so why was I even thinking about this girl?

"Nathan?"

Surprised, I turned as Mrs. Blackwell walked toward me. Where the hell had she come from? She was a nice lady, and I'd always liked her, especially considering she was a huge football fan. She didn't miss a Friday night game and sure liked to ride Coach when she didn't agree with a play.

I smiled. "Hey, Mrs. Blackwell. I'm okay to keep going, if that's all right with you."

She smiled back at me, and as I studied her, I realized exactly where Princess Monroe got her unusual eye color. Funny, I'd never noticed it before, but then again, it's not like I spent much time checking out anyone over the age of twenty-five. That would be weird.

"You most certainly will not. It's five o'clock, and you've been out here for hours." She glanced at the fence and her eyes softened some more. "It looks wonderful, Nathan."

For a moment, the two of us stared at the half-done fence that surrounded her family crypt. The iron had been forged into a pretty intricate design, and though I thought it was kinda creepy—keeping your family bones on the property—I wasn't about to judge anyone. Around these parts, a lot of folks did the same.

"All I did was slap some paint on it, Mrs. Blackwell. It's pretty hard to screw that up."

"I suppose." She smiled and turned back to me, her hands on her hips. "Your uncle called. He's been trying to get hold of you but your cell phone must be dead. He's still having problems at one of his work sites, so he won't be able to give you a lift home."

Her eyes settled on me with a clarity that made me uncomfortable. Of course she knew about that night. Of course she knew that I was suspended from driving. Everyone in the whole freaking parish knew about that night.

I thought of the fridge at home. It was full of Dad's beer, and I knew that if I locked myself away in the dark and took the time to get good and drunk, then maybe I wouldn't think about that night. I wouldn't care about the dark holes in my head. The ones that I'd been desperate to fill. The ones that shouldn't be there. The ones that would tell me why I'd been so damn stupid.

But for now, I just wanted to forget everything.

"Come have dinner with us—"

I started to protest. "No, really, Mrs. Blackwell, I'll just head home. I don't mind."

"Nathan Everets."

I stood a little straighter, because in my world, when a lady spoke at you like that, you paid attention.

"I know for a fact your parents are on holiday, and I'll bet you haven't had a proper meal all week."

"Honestly, I'm cool with working some more and heading home before dark."

I didn't want to see Monroe, and I sure as hell preferred to be by myself.

"It's not a bother, really, and after dinner, I'll have my granddaughter drive you home."

I shook my head, but she wouldn't listen, and five minutes later, I found myself in a small bathroom just off the kitchen, scrubbing the dirt and grime from my hands and trying to clean up as best I could.

My stomach rumbled as the smell of good old Louisiana barbecue wafted in from the kitchen.

"Better than the frozen crap at home," I muttered. My mom had made me a few casseroles, but they were still in the freezer where she'd left them. I'd been surviving on frozen pizza and burgers from The Grill whenever Link came to visit.

One last glance in the mirror told me it was as good as it was gonna get, so I tugged off my bandana and shoved it in my pocket, pulling out my cell as I did so. I turned it back on, and a quick glance told me Rachel had texted a few more times, the last one barely intelligible.

U cmign?

Guess the party was in full swing up at the cabin.

"Dinner's ready, Nathan."

I pushed the door open, and the first thing I saw was Monroe. She'd changed out of the tight little top she'd been wearing and the short shorts were gone too. Bummer, because even though she was a prickly little thing, the shorts were kinda hot. She placed a bowl of taters on the table and slid into her seat. She looked pale, paler than anyone I knew, but that could be a New York thing.

I thought of Rachel and her obsession with being tanned and skinny. It's all the girl talked about when she wasn't shoving beers down her throat and avoiding anything that wasn't green and leafy. I tried to explain once that beer and alcohol were just as bad as eating a Big Mac, but she laughed and said, "not when you puke it all up, it isn't."

Pretty hard to argue with that kind of logic.

Mrs. Blackwell sat down and passed a plate of barbecued chicken and ribs over to Monroe. Without skipping a beat, she grabbed a half rack and tossed it onto her plate before passing the platter along to me, her chin thrust forward as if waiting for me to say something.

Wow. They really did make them different in New York.

# Chapter Five

# Monroe

I wasn't happy to be sharing dinner with Captain Sweaty Pants and I wasn't sure why Gram thought it was a good idea. I guess she was just being polite, but I liked our low-key evenings. Dinner was done and the mess cleaned up by six. Gram changed into her comfortable clothes—I never seemed to get out of mine—and I read while she watched the Home and Garden channel. That was how it had been every night since I arrived.

There had been no fuss, no long involved conversations, and I hadn't had to pretend to be normal. Or happy.

I made a mental note to email my therapist later. Apparently I wasn't completely dead inside. There *were* things I cared about after all.

I liked quiet.

I liked simple.

I liked comfortable.

And the guy across from me was anything but those three things. He was one of those boys. One of the dark and complicated ones. He was a boy who could probably get any girl he wanted just by sliding a smile her way (a) because he had a nice smile, and (b) I was guessing a smile from him would make a girl think she was the only one he was looking at. A smile from him just might make her feel special.

Lucky for me, I didn't want anything to do with boys like him—you know, the complicated ones. I wasn't here at Gram's to socialize. In fact, I hated socializing.

About a month ago, my friend Kate had convinced me to go to a party at Blake Mathew's place. His parents were out of town and his older brother was home from college. It was supposed to be *the* summer kickoff party. I knew it was a mistake, but Kate had begged and I'd given in. At the time, I'd thought that maybe I was ready to move on. Maybe I was ready to be normal again.

I'd spent the entire night hiding in a dark corner, sipping the same warm beer. Any guy who approached was shot down because I had no idea how to act or what to say.

I studied my friends. I watched them laugh and have fun. I watched them dance and act crazy, and I watched them kiss and cuddle.

It made me furious. It made me sick…and it made me so sad. Because no matter how hard I tried to be that girl—to be the one who was light and happy, the one who my parents wanted back—I couldn't be her. I knew she didn't exist anymore, and I was pretty sure she was never coming back.

I frowned as I yanked on my top—the cami was long gone,

but the coral blouse I'd thrown on was a little snug across the chest. I'd also axed the shorts, because, well, they were way too short, opting for a jean skirt instead. The fact that I'd finally brushed out my hair had nothing to do with Nathan Everets, even though I could tell that's exactly what Gram was thinking.

But she'd be wrong. Way wrong.

Nathan, on the other hand, looked totally relaxed. He had tossed his bandana but covered up his muscles with a white T-shirt. It did nothing to hide the six-pack that I knew was underneath, mostly because it fit him like a second skin and was threadbare as if it had been washed many times. *The Cramps* spelled out across his chest in faded red letters.

Though it was rather presumptuous of me to claim the popular New York alternative band as my own, it bugged me that he even knew who they were. They were edgy and political, not hillbilly country blues.

I knew I was generalizing but couldn't seem to help myself.

I passed Nathan the platter of ribs, after throwing enough pork onto my plate to feed a small country. I wasn't even hungry, so what was up with that?

I took a sip of iced tea and glanced up at the clock, 5:15.

All I had to do was get through the next forty-five minutes, and then he would leave and I could go back to my totally inappropriate reading material—taken from my mother's night table—and get on with my quiet Friday night.

"So, Nathan, how is Trevor doing?"

Nathan choked on a rib. Or at least I think he did. I glanced from him and back to Gram, wondering at the odd expression that crept over his face.

He cleared his throat as Gram poured herself some iced tea before offering the jug to Nathan. He shook his head and stared down at his plate. "He's the same, I guess."

"I see," Gram replied softly.

I didn't.

"Who's Trevor?"

Nathan's head shot up, and the look in his eyes was so bleak that, for a moment, I forgot to breathe. His eyes were blue, dark blue like the Atlantic on a cold winter day, and at the moment, they were filled with something I was all too familiar with.

Pain. But not just pain. It was so much more.

Something inside me twisted, and a wave of nausea rolled through me.

"Sorry," I said quickly. "That was rude." I glanced at Gram and shook my head. "None of my business."

I tore some meat off a rib bone and shivered, suddenly cold. Sweat beaded along my brow, and even though I felt like I was freezing, it was, in fact, hot as hell in the house.

This weird roaring started in my ears—it was thick and pressed into me, so I knew I was already running to catch up. If I didn't get hold of my shit, Gram and Nathan would have a front-row seat to a one-of-a-kind freak-show panic attack.

I went through the steps my therapist had taught me.

I exhaled, fingers trailing through the condensation that gathered along the bottom of my glass as I tried to slow down. I counted, concentrating on the numbers, starting at twenty and working my way back. My chest hurt, but eventually my heart relaxed, and the pressure eased. It took a bit, but after a while, the fuzziness went away and everything became clearer.

It was then that I realized Nathan was staring at me as if I'd grown two heads and Gram's eyes were misty, her lined face drawn in concern.

"Are you all right, Monroe?" she asked carefully.

"I'm fine," I muttered and shoved a piece of meat into my mouth. I forced myself to chew it slowly and washed it down with a long, cold drink.

5:30. Nearly there.

I didn't say one word for the rest of the meal. I didn't really need to; Gram more than made up for the fact that Nathan wasn't in his happy place anymore and that I had never really gotten there.

I listened as Gram chatted about some kind of peach festival that was going on in Twin Oaks for the weekend while studying Nathan covertly. I didn't feel like talking, and he was more interesting than the rose pattern on Gram's wallpaper.

His brown hair was longer than it had looked underneath his bandana, and I could tell he spent a lot of time outdoors because his ends were lighter. When he turned his head, the pieces shimmered like warm butter, which really wasn't fair because I knew more than a few girls who laid down big bucks to achieve the same look.

With his blue eyes, square jaw, and hot body, there was no denying Nathan Everets was packing some pretty serious genes.

He smiled at Gram, and I could tell that she was charmed, but then how could she not be? He was polite, well-spoken, and really good-looking. I wondered if she sensed the darkness that ran just beneath the surface like I did. He was hiding stuff. I saw it, but then again, I guess that's no surprise since these days I was all about the darkness.

He made some comment—I couldn't tell you what they were talking about—and Gram laughed. She laughed like a schoolgirl, all deep-chested and animated and giddy. I wondered if Nathan was a player. Or if he had a girlfriend that he was faithful to. If so, I found it odd that on a Friday night, he was stuck making small talk with us instead of having fun with his friends.

He and Gram ate peach cobbler while discussing football, and my eyes glazed over. I hated football. I mean, really, what was the point in lining up across from some huge Neanderthal whose only mission was to kick your ass all over the place?

I didn't get it. When they started talking about some guy named Peyton, I couldn't take it anymore.

"So you like The Cramps," I asked, though it was more of a statement than a question, and judging by the look on Gram's face, it had come out sorta rude.

Nathan sat back in his chair and nodded. "Yeah, they're

awesome. The guitarist is old school and I appreciate that. Too many guys these days are just hacks. They wouldn't know what an arpeggio scale was if it hit them on the head."

"Really," I murmured. They weren't the only ones. What the heck was an arpeggio scale?

Gram sat up and grabbed the empty bowls off the table. "Nathan here is quite the musician."

Ah, now I understood the tattoos and hair. He wasn't just into the look; he was part of the scene.

Nathan's face hardened, and the darkness or sadness or whatever you wanted to call it was there again. It was in the blank expression that crept into his eyes, the way his hands froze, and the way his shoulders hunched forward as if trying to protect himself from something.

It made me wonder. From what?

"So you must be a guitarist," I said.

He shrugged and didn't answer. Instead he pushed his chair back and got to his feet. "Thanks a lot, Mrs. Blackwell, that was way better than what I had waiting for me at home."

Gram leaned against the counter. "Thanks for your hard work today, Nathan. You'll be back Monday, or will it be your uncle?"

He shoved his hands into his front pockets, and for a moment, I glimpsed the tops of his boxers again, along with a pretty impressive span of flat, toned skin. My cheeks flushed when I glanced up and realized he was watching me watching him.

A hint of a smile touched the corner of his mouth, and I didn't like the way his eyes glittered beneath the soft light from overhead.

He was arrogant, and I didn't like him.

Or maybe I didn't like how he made me feel, which was something I didn't want to think about. At least, not right now.

"I'm pretty sure I'm here for the next few weeks," he answered, his attention once more on Gram. I exhaled a long, hot breath and pushed at a few pieces of hair that stuck to my neck.

Gram smiled. "Wonderful." She paused, her eyes swinging my way, her forehead drawn thoughtfully. About a half a second before she spoke, I knew what she was up to. I opened my mouth in an effort to dodge the bullet, but she beat me to the punch.

"Do you have plans tomorrow afternoon, Nathan?"

Oh. My. God.

I gave Gram the stink eye but she ignored me, even with my right eyebrow raised at least an inch or more.

If Nathan was surprised by Gram's question, he sure didn't show it.

"Nope. Some of the guys are up at a cottage, and I'm stuck here, so…"

"I see," Gram said, still avoiding my glare.

I swear, if she goes where I think she's going to go—

"So, would you be able to take Monroe to the Peach Festival in town? She's been stuck with me for a week, and I'm not exactly exciting company for a sixteen-year-old."

"I'm almost seventeen," I interrupted.

Okay, Nathan seemed surprised now. He hunched his shoulders even more and rolled on the heels of his feet.

"Uh…"

Oh great. From the pained look on his face, I gathered that he'd rather eat rat poison than take me to some stupid Peach Festival.

Not that I wanted to go or anything, but still…something about the way he avoided looking in my general direction pissed me off.

"I'd for sure take Monroe, Mrs. Blackwell, but I…"

His face flushed deeply, and for a moment, I forgot to feel insulted, mostly because my curiosity was piqued. Something was up, and for the first time in a long time, I wanted to know what it was—probably because it wasn't me under the microscope. But still, my therapist would be fist-pumping right about now.

"I can't drive, so…I mean, I can drive, I'm just not allowed to, um, drive right now." Nathan said the words as if he could barely get them out. His eyes narrowed, like he was mad, and he looked at the floor.

Gram's face softened. "That's not a problem. Monroe can take my car."

What? Wait a second. She was going to let me drive her big boat?

I glanced out the window at the big beast, or what Gram

referred to as "the Matlock." I had no clue who or what a Matlock was, though she told me once he was a judge or an actor…or an actor judge. Who knows, but the car was long and silver and shiny, and did I say long? She was crazy to let me drive it.

"Oh," Nathan mumbled. "I guess that could work."

Gee, don't be all excited or anything.

"Thank you, Nathan," Gram said with a big, embarrassing smile on her face. Nothing like being pimped out by your own flesh and blood. "Do you want Monroe to give you a ride home tonight?"

"No," he answered quickly.

So quickly that I whipped my head up, no longer interested in the pretend piece of lint I was picking off my skirt. Okay, I knew I wasn't supermodel material or anything, but I wasn't dog meat either, so his attitude hit a nerve. The thing of it was I was surprised at my reaction.

"I could use a walk after eating all that food." Nathan glanced at me, and I hoped he could tell that I wasn't into this peach thing. It wasn't my fault that Gram was hopelessly looking for ways to—what had my therapist called it? Engage me. She wanted to bring me back to life and was willing to sell me to the local hottie to do it.

"Monroe will pick you up around four tomorrow, sound good?"

His eyes were still on me, so I thrust out my chin, though when his gaze wandered down to my chest—just for a second—my breath caught, and I hated the blush that stained my cheeks.

I could say no. I could ruin Gram's expectations that her granddaughter would have a great night. Or her hope that, finally, Monroe would snap out of the funk that was never ending. I could disappoint her and watch the light fade from her eyes. I could watch her smile disappear altogether. Lord knows I'd done it to my parents many times in the past year.

But I couldn't. Not with Gram. Besides, it would be worth it just to make Nathan as miserable at the thought of a night out with me as he obviously felt.

"Monroe?" Gram asked again, and I glanced toward her.

"I'll try and fit it into my schedule." I pushed my chair back and left.

Of course I didn't want to seem too eager or anything.

# Chapter Six
# Nathan

At two minutes after four, I watched Mrs. Blackwell's old Crown Vic make its way up my driveway. The thing was practically an antique, but man, she kept it mint. American-made and a pig on gas, the car had to be at least twenty feet long. And judging by the speed at which Monroe turned into our driveway, it would be lucky if it was returned to its owner without a ding or two.

She drove like a city girl, which would be one speed—fast—and it was obvious she didn't know how to corner the damn thing. I wasn't sure what Mrs. Blackwell was thinking letting Monroe drive, but then, it wasn't my car.

My jaw tightened as I glanced toward the garage. Toward the car that was mine. The one that was off limits.

Monroe pulled up and threw the Crown Vic into park, her eyes finding mine as she sat there for a moment. I wondered if she was as uncomfortable about this situation as I was.

It wasn't like it was a date or anything, and I wasn't sure if she knew that. I decided as I took the first step off the porch I was going to have to set Monroe straight on that point.

Technically, I still had a girlfriend. And even though I had decided sometime in the night—most likely between the twentieth and thirtieth pathetic, drunken text I had received from Rachel—that I was gonna call it quits as soon as she got back from the cottage, this thing with Monroe still wasn't a date.

I yanked on the passenger door, slid in beside her, and was immediately hit with the smell of…summer. Fresh, sweet summer.

I glanced at her in surprise, noticed that her hair was down, and again was hit with summer…and something else. Something heavier. Something I had no name for, but man, it was nice.

"Hey," I said, clearing my throat because suddenly there was a frog the size of a baseball lodged in my throat.

*God, you smell good.*

"Hey yourself," she replied as she reversed the car into a three-point turn. Once she had maneuvered the vehicle back down the driveway and turned right onto the road, she cleared her throat. "And just so you know? This isn't a date or anything. I don't date boys like you."

Okay, that got my attention, hard and fast. I glanced at her. I let my eyes roll over the mint-green halter top that did nothing to hide the curves this girl had. Her legs were smooth, trim, and athletic, and from where I was sitting, the white skirt she had on was on the short side. Hell yeah, was it ever. Her toes were painted green to match the halter top, her feet slipped into casual sandals.

At least the girl was practical when it came to shoes. Good to know. The last time I had taken Rachel to a music festival in the neighboring parish, she'd worn these four-inch platform things that (a) looked ugly as shit, and (b) hurt her feet so badly that I had to listen to her complain for freaking hours.

Shit. When Rachel and I had first started dating, it was all about being together—just hanging out at my place and getting to know each other. But the last year was more about how we looked when we were out together, and that got pretty old after a while. I wasn't sure what had changed, but there had been a time when Rachel was a lot of fun.

Or maybe it was me who had changed.

I pushed all thoughts of Rachel away and snuck a peek at Monroe.

Her hair was a mess of inky-black waves, and those eyes were as interesting as I remembered—so light they appeared almost clear—and her mouth…

Bingo.

This might not be a date, but she sure as hell was dressed for one.

My gaze rested there, on that perfect, lush, and glossy mouth, for a heartbeat—maybe longer. No girl put on that glossy shit and let her hair down unless she wanted to look good. And smell good.

I smiled.

She scowled and arched an eyebrow.

"A guy like me?" I settled back in my seat, indicating that she turn left. This would be good, I thought. "Should I be insulted?" I continued, thinking that I kinda sorta was.

"Don't take it personally, Romeo, but you're not my type," she said, a hint of rasp in her voice, as if there was something caught in her throat. Words, maybe?

"You have a type?"

"Don't you?" she shot back.

I shrugged but didn't answer.

"I'll bet your type is tall, blond, and tanned, but then, what do I know?"

That annoyed me. Mostly because she was right. But hey, in my defense, Rachel was a good time in addition to being real easy on the eyes, and she rocked a string bikini like no one's business. At least she used to. Hell, I'm sure she still did, it's just not something I noticed anymore.

She still wanted to drink and smoke weed and party, and I didn't. Not with her and not with anyone else.

"And you think this because…" I glared at her.

She made another weird sound, and I noticed that she gripped the steering wheel so hard her knuckles were white.

"Do you have a girlfriend?" she asked, eyes straight ahead on the road.

Shit. This was going to make me look bad. I could lie but that really wasn't my thing.

"Yeah, at the moment, I do."

"At the moment?" She laughed and muttered, "Unreal."

"It's not what it sounds like," I retorted, pissed off that she'd managed to piss me off minutes into our non-date.

"I'm sure it's not."

"Look, I don't know what your story is, and I really don't care. In case you forgot, it was your grandmother who arranged this little whatever the hell it is, not me. So get over yourself."

"Whatever," she muttered.

"Besides," I continued, feeling a wave of heat rush through me, one that was full of anger. "You're right about one thing."

She slowed down as we approached the city limits. "Oh yeah, Romeo, what's that?"

"I do have a type, and you're not it."

"Ouch," she replied sarcastically, eyes on the road ahead.

"I can't imagine with that attitude you'd be anyone's type."

She had no comeback for that one, and I exhaled, sinking into my seat as I stared out the window. I thought that maybe it was going to be the longest afternoon of my life.

We reached the festival grounds about five minutes later. After Monroe refused to take money off me for parking, we headed into the Peach Festival, one that I hadn't attended since I was, like, twelve.

As we headed into the main area, I remembered why. It was for kids. I looked around and sighed. Old people and kids. *Lots* of old people and kids.

There was a midway near the back. I could see the Ferris

wheel from where we stood, and game alley was set up just in front. Between us and the midway was a huge number of arts and craft booths, and beyond that were food stands.

"You want something to eat?" I grumbled, wanting nothing more than to end this thing as quickly as I could. I figured if I shoved some food into her and toured the grounds quickly, we could call it a night and be done with it.

"Sure," she said. "In a bit. I want to look at the craft booths, if that's all right?"

I glanced down at her sharply, but she stared straight ahead. It was then that I realized a few things. She was small next to me, probably five-four, while I was a couple of inches over six feet and still growing. With her pale skin, pale eyes, and dark hair, she really was the opposite of Rachel or any other girl I'd ever dated.

There was something about her though. I couldn't put my finger on it, but I thought that maybe if I wasn't so screwed up and she wasn't such a bitch, she could be someone I'd be interested in.

Maybe.

"Oh, look," she pointed toward a booth. "Rag dolls."

I groaned and followed her into the craft center.

*Maybe not.*

# Chapter Seven

# Monroe

*"You're right about one thing. I do have a type, and you're not it."*

Ouchie.

Or at least it would be an ouchie if I cared. Which I didn't. Not really. I was used to people backing away from me. It was usually in response to me opening my mouth and saying something nasty, which was easy enough to do when your parents were just grateful that you spoke at all.

I knew I'd been a bitch in the past, just as I'd been right now. I just couldn't seem to help myself.

And sure, my therapist told me it was my way of keeping my distance—of avoiding contact, but whatever. For the most part, I preferred to be alone, which was why this whole festival thing was stupid.

I grabbed my peach sundae and chose a seat as far away from anyone as I could. I didn't do crowds real well, so for the hundredth time, I asked myself why I had let Gram manipulate me into this evening with Nathan.

Nathan followed and slid into the chair opposite me and smiled at some girl who shouted at him from the cotton candy stand.

I filled my mouth with way too much sugar and glanced over to the girl who held hands with a boy as they walked by. Her eyes lingered on me for several seconds, and then she whispered something into her boyfriend's ear. He turned, nodded at Nathan, and then stared at me for so long I raised an eyebrow and stared right back.

He smiled.

She yanked on her boyfriend's arm and pulled him toward the midway, but not before she got her bitch on, raised her eyebrows in return, and flipped me a mental bird.

I smirked and shoved another spoonful of sundae into my mouth. I wanted her to know that her attitude didn't bother me.

But it did. And that was something new too. What the hell?

"Why are you here?" Nathan asked as he scooped a good amount of peaches and whipped cream into his mouth.

"Um, because Gram made me?"

His blue eyes settled on me, and there was nowhere to hide. He sat back in his chair and studied me intently, his eyes so clear they reminded me of the summer sky. For a moment, I forgot that I didn't like him.

He grinned, and I glanced down at my dessert, exhaling hard as a rush of heat rolled through me.

"That's not what I meant. Why are you here in Louisiana with your grandmother?"

Panic hit me—it froze everything inside me—but then I did what I always did. I deflected.

"Why was your driver's license suspended?"

His smile disappeared, and his eyes narrowed in a way that told me everything. His shoulders hunched forward and he frowned.

"Is this what we're going to do? Play a stupid game?" He paused and then pushed his sundae away.

I watched him in silence, and though the last thing I wanted to do was eat, I shoved another spoonful of the melting crap into my mouth. At least this way, I couldn't open it and make things worse.

Another shout of "Hey Nate," slid between us, but he didn't bother to look up—he just stared down at the table like it was the most interesting thing in the world. I forced myself to swallow the ice cream—it was either that or puke—and then I pushed my bowl away as well.

I was about to apologize, something I didn't do much of these days, but when I opened my mouth to speak, he glanced up, and the words I was about to say, two simple little words, *I'm sorry*, died in my throat.

Nathan Everets looked exactly the way I felt most of the time. He looked haunted. Sort of…broken.

He pushed a long strand of hair off his face, his eyes never leaving mine. "I can't drive because I was involved in an accident three months ago. A bad one."

"Oh," I managed to get out. "Look, you don't have to…"

Shit, I didn't want to do this with him. I didn't want him to share with me, because then he'd expect me to share back, and there was no way in hell I wanted anyone to know anything about me. Period.

I couldn't talk about Malcolm. *I couldn't.*

"I left a party with my best friend, Trevor, and our girlfriends."

And yet I was helpless to stop him. Helpless to look anywhere other than into his eyes, because for some reason, the pain that I saw there let me know I wasn't the only one…

*I wasn't the only one who hated herself.*

Nathan shook his head, and that piece of hair fell back across his cheek. I found myself focusing on it, watching as it lifted in the slight breeze and tickled the edge of his nose.

"I don't remember driving. I don't remember getting into the car." He leaned forward now, his voice louder. Angrier. "That's how incredibly stupid I was. Me. The guy who was supposed to stay sober. Clean."

"I drove Trevor's car down State Route 9, and somewhere between the party and the old Dixon farm, I wrapped it around a hydro pole."

He kept clenching and unclenching his fist.

"I only broke my left pinky finger, if you can believe it, and other than a few bruises and cuts from flying glass, I was good to go. The girls were okay too, a few minor scratches but nothing serious. We were all knocked out, but Trevor…" His voice trailed off and he finally glanced away.

It was then that I realized I'd been holding my breath.

"You don't, you don't have to…I don't want to know," I whispered. And suddenly I didn't. I didn't want to know anything about Nathan Everets and this Trevor guy.

He shoved away from the table suddenly. "Let's get out of here."

I followed Nathan through the crowd, half running to keep up with him, but then maybe he was trying to get away from me. He finally stopped near the edge of the midway, and the sounds, the laughter was so loud that I turned away and faced craft alley.

We were surrounded by families, by teenagers and kids who were having a blast. They were laughing and shouting, and why shouldn't they? What was not to like? If you were into peaches, that is. There was every kind of dessert imaginable, rides and games, and over on the other side, I saw a stage with instruments, drums and guitars. So there was entertainment too.

There was everything that most normal people needed to have a good time. Except I wasn't normal, and the more smiling faces I saw, the angrier I got.

It wasn't fair.

"I wish they would shut up."

"Huh?" Nathan glanced down at me, his hands shoved into his pockets, his expression blank.

"Everyone." I gestured toward the Ferris wheel. "Everything. It's too loud."

His cell dinged, for the twentieth time, and I snapped. "Aren't you going to answer that?"

Nathan grabbed his phone and glanced down at it.

I assumed it was his girlfriend, his "at the moment girlfriend," and I looked away in disgust, my eyes falling upon a cotton candy stand. A little boy who looked to be six or seven was in line for a stick, smiling up at his dad as the two of them waited. When the lady handed him his prize, the vibrant pink color caught my attention.

For a few moments, it was all I saw. Pink. Fluffy. The little boy.

Sweat trickled down the back of my neck, and I lifted a heavy chunk of hair and pulled it forward over my shoulder. I couldn't take my eyes off the treat, and when the little boy dug in, his mouth grabbing for the biggest piece he could get, I wanted to yell at him.

*Be careful. You'll get that crap in your hair, and then your mother will be mad, and then I'll have to...*

"Monroe, are you all right?"

"What?" I shook my head and exhaled a long, shaky breath. I thought of my bed. Of the pills I no longer had. And I glanced down at my wrist, at the single, solitary scar that was there. It wasn't big and it wasn't flashy. Kind of like me.

It was a testament to the real me. The weak part. The part that couldn't do anything right.

"Monroe?"

"I hate it here," I said quietly.

Nathan glanced at his cell one more time, his long fingers

running over the screen. "If I ask you to take me somewhere, will you?"

"You're not some kind of criminal, are you?" I thought of his suspension and realized I didn't know much of anything about him.

"Nope," he answered. "Not the kind you need to be afraid of, anyway."

My gaze returned to the little boy whose face was all but swallowed by the large stick of cotton candy, and I knew if I stayed, I would be sick.

"Sure," I said and took a step forward, "as long as you promise there aren't any rides, games, or peaches."

*Or kids.*

"I promise," he said as he fell in step beside me.

For the first time today, I relaxed a bit. "So, where are we going?"

We were almost to the parking lot when he answered, his voice not only subdued and maybe distracted but definitely sad.

"The hospital."

Wait. What?

That wasn't what I had expected to hear. A party maybe. Or an underage club—if they had them out here in the boonies—but the hospital?

And yet, the sea of happy that existed here at the Peach Festival was so thick I felt like I was drowning. Even though I hated hospitals, I couldn't deny that, at the moment, they were more my speed.

Anyplace other than here was where I wanted to be. "Okay," I answered. "Let's go."

# Chapter Eight

# Nathan

I stared at the text again, my heart pounding so hard I was sure Monroe heard it. **They're gone for now. Can you make it?**

Did I want to? Did I want to make it?

"Turn left at the lights."

We passed Sheriff Bellafonte's car parked next to the bus stop and I looked away, glad that Monroe's lead foot was relaxing a bit. Up ahead, I saw the hospital, and I told Monroe where to park for free, on Fraser Street just to the right. She pulled in along the sidewalk, and I pretended not to notice when she bumped the curb.

Foo Fighters were playing on the radio, and the air that blew from the vents was colder than I liked. Guess the northern girl wasn't used to our steamy summers, but I liked the heat.

I blew out a long, hot breath, my foot tapping an insane beat on the floor. I was nervous, and I felt like my head was going to explode, but I kept it cool. I had to.

"Are you going to be long?" Monroe asked.

She tapped her fingers along the steering wheel, and when she turned to look at me, for one second—for one perfect second—I thought she had the most beautiful eyes I'd ever seen.

"Nathan?" she asked.

"Call me Nate," I said as I reached for the door handle.

"What?"

"Nate," I said again and opened the door. "It's what my friends call me. Nathan is saved for the parents and everyone else."

I rounded the car and stared down at her.

"So we're friends now?" she said, her fingers still tapping the steering wheel, tap, tap, tap, in rapid succession.

"Are you coming?" I asked instead, moving back so she could open the door. She hadn't even asked why I was here or what I was going to do, which I found interesting. I wondered if it was because she was afraid to ask, but then I decided it was more that she didn't give a crap. She wasn't exactly the warm and fuzzy type, and I guess that was another thing that I kinda sorta liked about her.

She wasn't clingy or needy or begging me for something that I couldn't give her. It was nice to be with someone who had no expectations.

Just last week, Rachel had gotten all heavy on me, afraid that I was mad at her about something and that I was going to break up with her. She begged me to tell her that everything was going to be all right, and I gave in.

But the lie still stuck in my throat, and when I thought about it, I felt sick.

Monroe glanced behind me, toward the hospital. I'm sure she thought I was a freak. Hell, I probably was. What kind of guy brings a girl to the hospital? A girl he hardly knows? And yet, I needed her. I needed *someone*, and I guess it sucked for Monroe that she was the only person around.

"Come on," I repeated, my hand held out.

I could pour on the charm. Smile a certain way and lean against the car. Stare into her eyes like she was the most important girl in the world. I knew what girls liked, and I also knew what I could get away with. But I didn't think any of that would work with this particular girl. Her bullshit meter seemed to be sharp.

So I waited. And I hoped she couldn't tell that I was basically shitting my pants at the thought of going in there by myself.

"You're weird," she said softly.

"Promise you won't tell anyone?" I smirked.

She shook her head, but there was a slight smile around the corner of her mouth, and for some reason, it felt good to know I'd put it there.

I stepped back, and she opened her door.

We headed up Fraser to the corner and waited for the light to change. When it did, I grabbed her hand—an automatic thing—and was surprised that she let me.

I was also really surprised at how small and soft her hand was. She didn't have those fake four-inch things that Rachel and a lot of her girlfriends had. Shit, you could poke a guy's eyes out if you weren't careful. And I didn't want to think about how many times I'd had to listen to Rachel and her friends bitch about breaking one of them.

In the grand scheme of things, I didn't care about something as stupid as fake nails, and I was willing to bet most of my buddies didn't either.

But her hand didn't stay in mine for long, and by the time we reached the entrance, I reluctantly gave in to her gentle tugs and released her.

She followed me to the elevators, and I punched the fifth floor as if I had every right to. As if I'd done it a thousand times before, when I'd only been up there once and that had been a disaster.

Monroe didn't say anything, she just followed me inside the elevator, and I wished her hand was still in mine because honestly, the urge to bolt was bad.

I thought of Rachel and how she had refused to come with me that first time, three months ago. She'd pulled out the big guns, had cried until her mascara made raccoon tracks down her cheeks, and she'd managed to make me feel worse than I already did. So I went without her, and it had turned out pretty much the way she thought it would.

It had sucked. If she knew I was here now, I'm sure she'd hit me in the shoulder and call me a loser.

But she wasn't. I glanced down at my empty hand, and I was still staring down when the elevator doors slid open.

The first thing I saw was the nurse's station. The second? Taylor's fierce scowl and her wild, blond hair.

"Who the hell is that?" she pointed at Monroe.

"You don't need to be such a bitch, Taylor. This is Monroe. She's just a…a friend."

"Uh-huh," she said. "So she's your ride?" I knew she was thinking about Rachel, and judging by the nasty look she gave Monroe, she thought there was a whole lot more going on between us.

"Yeah," I answered, a little pissed at her attitude. "What else would she be?"

Monroe muttered something under her breath, and I guess I was glad I didn't hear it, because I had the feeling it wasn't nice. "I'll be waiting over there," she pointed toward a tired-looking lounge just past the nurse's station. "You know, when you need your *ride* home."

Shit. She was pissed too. Seemed as if I was on a roll.

"Monroe," I said softly.

"Forget it, *Nathan*. Go and do whatever it is you need to do, but I'm not sticking around all night."

I watched her cross over to the lounge. Watched her sit on the sofa, a faded brown one that looked like it was leather but I knew was cold, slippery vinyl. She ignored me, grabbed a magazine, and turned the other way, making me feel like an even bigger shit.

"Are you coming?" Taylor grabbed my arm. "They'll be back

soon, and if you get caught, my ass will be toast, and I don't even want to know what he'll do to yours."

Taylor led me down the hall even though she didn't need to. I remembered the way. I saw it in my nightmares.

He was still in the same room, and as we walked by the nurse's station, Taylor waved to them, which was a good thing, because I was pretty sure they wouldn't let me in on my own.

When we reached 514, Taylor paused and shoved her hands into the front pockets of her jeans. She looked tired, and the heavy black crap she put around her eyes didn't do much to help. A year younger than Trevor and I, she was like a kid sister to me.

"I'll let you," she mumbled and glanced down the hall before clearing her throat, "have some time."

I followed her gaze and caught Monroe looking our way. She stared at me for a few seconds and then flicked open her magazine again and disappeared behind it.

"Taylor, thanks."

When she looked back to me, her brown eyes were filled with tears, and something inside me broke. I did this to her. I thought of her family. I did this to all of them.

"You don't have long. They went for dinner at the Warehouse, and their reservation was for seven." She cleared her throat. "It's seven-thirty now, so that gives you about an hour before Mom and Dad will be back, 'cuz you know, we live at the freaking hospital now, so…"

"Thanks," I said quietly.

She didn't say anything. She just turned and leaned against the wall, her raccoon eyes closed, her breathing heavy.

The door slid open and I slipped inside, exhaling through my mouth because I hated the smell so much. The sick, stale, antiseptic smell that Trevor and his family lived with every single damn day.

The lights were low, and I turned toward the bed. Toward the machines and tubes and IV. Toward the big gray one that forced air into Trevor's lungs and then sucked it back out. The one that allowed him to breathe. The one that allowed him to live.

I swallowed hard and stared at the machine that allowed Trevor to exist in some weird, in-between place. I wondered if he knew I was there. Was he hanging out, levitating below the ceiling, staring down at the idiot who had put him here?

Carefully I made my way over to him, one foot in front of the other as if I was creeping across the foyer in my house after a night of partying.

It was stupid, really. What was I afraid of? That Trevor would wake up? No, that's what we all wanted. It was the stuff that came after that had me tied up in knots.

What if he told me to go screw myself and never come back? What if he told me that he hated me?

Or even worse, what if he woke up and couldn't say the things I knew were inside his head?

I paused at the edge of his bed. I took a moment to just look down at my best friend, and what I saw made my gut churn. It churned so badly that for a second I thought I was going to be sick, and it took everything I had to push the nausea away.

He'd lost a lot of weight and his hair was still shaved from when they'd cut into his skull to relieve the pressure because his brain had swelled a few days after the accident.

Funny thing was? Take away the tubes and shit and he kinda looked badass.

"Jesus, Trevor," I whispered.

A shiver rolled over me, and I crossed my arms over my chest, trying to find some heat. "Dude, you gotta wake up."

I leaned forward and touched his hand. It was cold, his skin almost papery and too soft for a guy. Even the colors in his wristband tattoo seemed faded and lost. The one on his shoulder? The tattoo that matched mine? I couldn't look at it.

Courage. Protection. That's the Celtic meaning behind the ink and obviously it was all a bunch of crap.

I stared down at my best friend and I wanted to cry like a baby. If he was here right now—really here—he'd headlock me, knock me on the chin, and call me a pussy. He'd say something stupid like, *It's better to live fast and die young, asshole.*

"I wish it had been me," I whispered hoarsely, wiping at my eyes angrily as I stood back and shoved my hands into my pockets.

I'm not sure how long I stood there like a stalker, just staring down at him, but I was surprised when Taylor yanked on my arm. Hard.

"Hey," I snapped, but my voice died when I caught sight of her eyes.

"You gotta get out of here. Mom texted from the lobby and they're on their way. Someone screwed up their reservations and they got sick of waiting, so they grabbed pizza or something." Taylor was frantic, and I knew how much of a line she'd crossed by letting me in to see her brother. "You gotta go, like, yesterday, Nate. I'm serious. I don't know what Dad will do if…"

"Shit." I glanced back at Trevor and then followed Taylor out of the room.

"Take the stairs, Nathan."

"I can't leave without Monroe." I paused near the nurse's station, trying to get Monroe's attention, but her head was still buried in her magazine.

"Oh my God, Nate. Forget about her. I'll tell her you had to leave and you can hook up with her later." She pushed me toward the stairs. "My dad will kill—"

"Nathan Everets."

I stared into Taylor's eyes, feeling the world slide away at the sound of her father's voice.

"I'm sorry," she mouthed, her eyes huge with worry as she glanced behind me at her parents.

You know that moment when your world is about to implode? That moment where you have to face a truth so hard you know it will knock you on your ass and you feel sick inside?

Yeah, I'm there right now, and as I turned back, it was all I could do to meet Mike Lewis's eyes. He used to like me. A lot. Hell, I spent more time at the Lewis place than my own, because Mike loved music as much as me and Trevor did, and he let us play as long and as loud as we wanted to.

Or I had. Past tense.

God, everything was so screwed up.

Trevor's dad is built like a Mack truck. He's six foot six with broad shoulders and arms that are covered in tattoos. His thick neck and square jaw are intimidating, but then so are the shaved head and bulging biceps.

A sob sounded just behind him and I felt sick all over again at the sad, forlorn look in Trevor's mom's eyes. Brenda Lewis was about the same age as my mom, but she looked at least ten years older now.

I guess not knowing if your kid is going to live will do that to you.

"I told you never to show your face here again," Mike said slowly, *carefully*, as if he was talking to an idiot. Which I guess he was.

He took a step toward me, and every muscle in my body ached with tension. My hands clenched and my chest tightened, and for one crazy second, I wished he would just throw a punch. Just one, because I needed to hurt more than I already did.

"Dad, leave him alone. He just wanted to see Trevor." Taylor tried to play nice, but her father wasn't having any of it. His eyes narrowed as they left me and moved to his daughter.

"You stay out of this. I'll deal with you at home." Mike's anger was so thick and strong, I swear you could see it in the air.

And I was choking on it. God, was I choking on it.

"Sir," I began, desperate to help, to do something, *anything* to defuse the situation. "This isn't Taylor's fault."

"I know," he said slowly, the veins in his neck corded and sticking out like something bad was filling them up. Hatred, most likely.

"This is your fault, Nathan. All of it." He pointed down the hall. "The fact that my boy is in there, lying in a coma, fighting for his life, that's on you." He sucked in a huge breath like he was about to dive underwater. "The fact that they had to cut into his skull so he didn't die, *that* is on you."

"Mike," Brenda said softly.

I was aware that everyone was watching. The nurses. The patients. The doctors. The man in his bright pink pajamas over by the elevators. It seemed as if everyone had stopped doing whatever it was they'd been doing and all eyes were on me.

"I'm not going to tear him apart, honey," Mike replied. "Even though I want to. But I'm telling you this now, man-to-man. I don't want to ever see you here again, got that? You nearly killed my son, and as far as I'm concerned, your ass should be in jail. We all know the only reason you're not riding a bench in juvie is because your daddy's got the mayor's ear and your uncle is an auxiliary officer in the sheriff's department."

"Sir…if I could trade places with Trevor, I would." The words tumbled from my mouth and I stepped forward.

He shook his head—a warning—and I stopped.

"I trusted you, Nathan. You were the responsible one, and maybe I was wrong to do that, but…I did, and I can't have you here right now because I can't control the anger I feel. Trevor's fighting for his life because of you."

His words ripped into me like a knife through bone. Every single one of them hurt.

Mike slipped his hands around his wife and hugged her, motioning for Taylor to join them. "Maybe I'm wrong to put this all on you but I can't help it. It's the way I feel and as much as the sight of you makes me sick." His voice was hoarse and he pointed down the hall. "What you saw in there? My son hooked up to a bunch of machines and tubes? That isn't something I'd wish on anyone, not even if they deserved it."

Mr. Lewis turned away from me, but he paused before heading back to Trevor's room. "I'm going to let this one slide, but if I see you up here again, I won't be so accommodating."

Taylor joined her parents, and I watched until they disappeared into Trevor's room. Suddenly my insides twisted so much that I bent over, hands on my knees, eyes closed. If I didn't get my shit together, I was going to be sick or I was gonna pass out.

A minute passed. Maybe more. And when I finally opened my eyes again, I saw mint-green toes.

"Okay, you win."

Slowly I straightened, my stomach recoiling but strong enough that I knew I wasn't going to puke. "Yeah?"

Monroe nodded and grabbed my hand, forcing me toward the elevators.

"Yep," she said as she pressed the lobby button. "You're officially the most pathetic person I know."

"Great. Thanks for that," I retorted sarcastically. Who the heck was she to talk like she knew what I was going through? As if she knew what it felt like to nearly die from regret and remorse and guilt?

"Just so you know, all it takes is one mistake to claim the crown, so watch out," I snapped.

The doors slid open and we stepped inside. Once they were closed, Monroe glanced up at me, her eyes huge and glassy. Her chest rose and fell, her lips were parted, and I smelled that summer scent again.

She held my gaze until the elevator doors slid open again and then she whispered, so softly that I barely heard, "At least your mistake is still alive."

# Chapter Nine

# Monroe

I couldn't believe I'd opened my mouth and let something like that slip out. What the hell was wrong with me?

*"At least your mistake is still alive."*

Was I crazy? Why the heck would I say something like that?

My heart pounded, so hard that I felt each beat pulse at the base of my neck, and I blew out a long breath as I slid into the car and waited for Nate to do the same. It was a few minutes after eight, and the sun was just starting to get real low in the sky. Red and gold streaked across the horizon, and I supposed it was pretty, but at the moment, I didn't give a shit about pretty.

At the moment, I was afraid that Nate would ask me what I meant, and if he did, I wasn't sure what I was going to say. I didn't talk about Malcolm. Ever.

I squeezed my eyes shut when I heard the passenger door squeak open. In an hour, it would be dark, but the darkness couldn't come soon enough for me because it was so much easier to hide.

I wanted to disappear. I wanted to melt into a puddle of nothing and pretend that I hadn't just opened my mouth and said what I'd said.

Nate slid in beside me and I cranked the Foos, wincing when Dave Grohl's voice cut through the silence.

*Why you'd have to go and let it die.* Pretty much perfect song right about now.

I pretended that everything was fine and normal. I pretended that I hadn't just seen Trevor's father rip Nate a new one. I pretended that I hadn't felt something when I'd looked into Nate's eyes.

But mostly I pretended that I hadn't just opened up my mouth and shared something with a boy I barely knew. *At least your mistake is still alive…* Shit.

It was hard though—to act like everything was cool. To kinda sorta smile through the lump that clogged my throat. But I did it. I did it because I had to. Because I didn't know how to be any other way.

*How the hell had Nate managed to get that out of me when it had taken my therapist nearly five months to get me to say a single freaking word?*

Maybe Nate hadn't heard. Maybe my brain was so screwed up that I thought I said something when, in fact, it was just the ghost of a whisper in my ear.

I turned the key all the way and revved Matlock a bit as I glanced into the rearview mirror and then into the side mirror.

I looked everywhere but at the guy beside me, because inside, I was counting. I was counting and trying like hell to focus.

One. Two. Three. Over and over again.

It was a good minute or so before I felt calm enough to glance his way, but when I did, my heart nearly popped out of my chest.

His dark eyes were on me. And they knew. *They knew.* They knew something bad had happened. Something worse than bad. Something unforgivable.

We stared at each other for a long time, so long that my eyes began to burn and I was afraid I was going to cry.

Wow. That would be epic.

"I can't talk about it," I said, grateful that the lump in my throat loosened.

Nate's eyes never left mine, and I shivered when he spoke, so soft and low that I don't think I actually heard him—I think that I read his lips. "Okay."

A long shuddering breath escaped me, and I put the car into gear.

"I don't want to go home yet," I said, staring ahead. My palms were sweaty, and even though it was hot as sin, I was shivering.

"Just drive."

I pulled out into the road and asked, "Where?"

Nate didn't answer. He pointed when he wanted me to turn right or left, and within ten minutes, we were on the outskirts of town. I didn't say anything because I honestly didn't care where we went as long as I didn't have to go back to Oak Run

Plantation. I couldn't explain the feeling that pressed into my chest any more than I could explain the need to be with Nate.

And that's what this was, wasn't it? I didn't want to be alone. Not now. Not tonight. Already images and sounds were crowding my brain, and it was all I could do to keep the stupid car on the road.

I didn't want to remember. Jesus, I didn't want to go back there.

"Take this right," Nate said, leaning closer as he gazed into the distance.

The sun was starting to set over the trees that lined the road, and for a moment, my eyes were blind as I navigated the turn. When the sun disappeared momentarily, I noticed a huge sign that looked like it was a hundred years old or something. Faded letters spread across it, broken in places. Damaged and worn. Kind of like me.

*Twin Oaks Drive-In.*

"Keep going," Nate urged.

A rusted gate was off to the side, and I snuck a look at him as I slowly drove up a large hill. His eyes were focused ahead, and I couldn't tell if he was nervous or pissed off or…or just nothing.

We crested the hill, and I saw a large screen, or rather the shell of what used to be a large screen, across a huge field littered with broken electrical or stereo hook-ups. This was an ancient drive-in, kind of like the one from that movie my mom liked to watch, *Grease.*

And it was deserted.

With the sun falling behind the tops of the trees that seemed to be everywhere, it was also kind of creepy.

"So why are we here?" I asked.

"Just keep driving. Take the path to the right."

He should know by now that I didn't like being told what to do, but considering the shitty night he'd had so far, I was willing to let this slide. "We aren't doing anything illegal, are we? Like is this trespassing or something?"

Nate shook his head and pointed. Trees surrounded the entire area like a blanket, and what used to be a food stand was missing its roof and all of its windows. Chipped paint dressed the doors and crumbling façade, and the shadows were long near the entrance.

I followed the path, noticing the worn grooves from tires, and didn't stop even when we entered the woods, though I did slow down.

"Up there," Nate said.

I glanced ahead and saw that the trees thinned. I also saw what looked like fire throwing shadows through the branches, and as we drove into a clearing, I spied several vehicles.

My heart thudded.

I saw about twenty kids hanging around the fire, drinking, laughing, jostling around. They looked like they were having a good time. Like nothing was wrong and everything was right.

I pulled in beside a huge, mud-splattered SUV because there was nowhere else to park and then cut the engine.

"Are those your friends?"

Nate nodded but didn't say anything. I didn't really want to be here, but I wasn't sure how to tell him.

"Is your girlfriend there?" I asked instead.

"No."

The tightness in my chest eased a bit, but it only managed to irritate me. Why was I so concerned about his girlfriend? It's not like this—us—was anything. This was just…I rapped my fingers along the top of the steering wheel, frustrated and pissed off and not really knowing why.

This was nothing. Nate was nothing. I was nothing.

We were caught up in nothing. Together.

"Come on, let's go."

Nate had his door open and was out of the car before I could say anything, and for a second, I thought of driving away. Of leaving him here and just driving into the night. Going somewhere far where I didn't have to think about Nathan or Trevor or Malcolm, or any of the mistakes we'd made to get to where we were.

"Are you coming?"

He poked his head inside the car, and though there was still this sort of sadness around his eyes, there was also something else. I thought that maybe that something else looked good on him. Maybe I was the reason that something else was there.

My mouth was dry and I tried to swallow. "Why are we here?" I managed to say.

He stared at me for so long without speaking that I felt my cheeks flush hot, and I wanted to look away, but I couldn't. That something else in his eyes touched me inside, and for just this one moment, it felt better than the nothing that was usually there.

He closed his door, and I watched him walk around the front of the car until he was beside mine. Carefully he yanked it open and moved aside so that I had room to move.

"You said you didn't want to go home yet." He paused. "I don't want to go home yet either."

Nate offered me his hand, and before I could stop myself, I took it. His warmth seeped into my cold fingers and his thumb pressed against the inside of my wrist.

My breath caught as I stared down at his hands.

His fingers were long and tapered, and I noticed a cool leather bracelet around his wrist. It looked old and weathered, as if he'd worn it for a long time. It meant something to him. Was it a gift from his girlfriend?

His thumb moved once more, his pad a little rough against my skin. The world tipped a little off center, and for one crazy second, time seemed to stop.

"Let's go," he said roughly, his thumb circling around until eventually he let go and turned toward the fire. "We won't stay late. Only until…"

"Until what?" I asked, taking the few steps needed until I was beside him.

Nate glanced down at me, his expression unreadable, but I saw the way his pulse pounded at the base of his neck. I saw it and felt it.

"Nate?"

"Maybe, for a little while, we can both forget."

Okay.

That was good enough for me.

## Chapter Ten

# Nathan

I didn't know if bringing Monroe out here was a good idea—heck, I didn't know if *me* being here was a good idea—but it sure felt right.

Though I suppose if my parents or uncle or even Mrs. Blackwell knew that I'd brought Monroe to a bush party, they wouldn't exactly be thrilled. But the party was low key and none of the hardcore guys were out yet. It was way too early. They didn't usually hit a party until after midnight, and I planned to be long gone by then.

I just wanted to…shit, I didn't know what I wanted to do. I only knew that I didn't want to be alone and I didn't know where else to go.

"Come on," I said again, and this time when I grabbed her hand, I didn't let go.

We started forward, and I nodded at a few guys tapping the keg over by an old tree stump. They shoved their red cups in the air and started to chug. There were a few more guys from the football team gathered around, and though they seemed happy to see me, none of them came over. I was used to that these days. No one seemed to know what to say.

Though I caught a few looks that landed on Monroe and didn't leave. Bill Ferris gave a long, low wolf whistle which Monroe ignored.

We reached the fire, and Monroe tugged her hand from mine. It was the right call. I mean, already a couple of girls who ran in Rachel's crowd were staring her down, but still, it felt good holding her hand.

*She* felt good. Steady. Real.

And that was pretty screwed up, considering I didn't think she liked me all that much, and technically, I still had a girlfriend.

I decided not to think about it too much. I decided that tonight I was gonna push all the crap out of my head and maybe have a good time. Or at least try to.

I'd been closed off from everyone for so long that it felt weird to see some of the old crowd hanging out near the fire, including Brent, the bassist in my band.

I thought he'd gone up to the cottage with Link and Rachel and the others, so it was a surprise to see him here.

He was shirtless, with his beige cargos hung so low I hoped he'd at least taken the time to pull on a pair of boxers. You see, Brent had a trigger. An old Def Leppard song, "Foolin'," was his dad's favorite song, and whenever he heard it, if he was drunk enough, off came his clothes.

The girls didn't seem to mind too much, and us guys just thought he was crazy as shit. Brent was also one hell of a wide receiver and, as quarterback, my go-to when we played. He had nimble fingers for catching my passes and made the bass sound melodic in a way that not many players could.

His face made me think of things I wanted to forget, but I couldn't lie.

It was good to see him.

"Dude," he said with a slow grin, grabbing my shoulders tightly as he shook me. "Where you been hiding yourself?"

We hadn't jammed once since the accident. Hell, I hadn't picked up my guitar since our last gig. And it wasn't that we couldn't or didn't want to. It's just…without Trevor, the band was dead. It was like the soul, the groove, and the life were gone, sleeping beside him in that hospital bed.

"I've been working for my uncle."

"Every damn day? That sucks."

For a moment, his bright blue eyes shadowed and he stood back, rubbing the day-old stubble along his jaw. It wasn't stubble so much as peach fuzz, and it was something I used to razz him about a lot.

Except I didn't feel much like razzing.

"You seen Trev?" he asked carefully.

I nodded but didn't elaborate. I wasn't about to tell him that Mike Lewis had just threatened to kick my ass all over the hospital. It was a small town. I'm sure he'd hear it soon enough.

"I stopped in a few weeks back but he just…" Brent's voice was subdued.

A heartbeat passed. Then another.

"Yeah, I know."

Brent's eyes quickly slid from me to Monroe and the moment passed. He winked at her. "New blood? What's your name, gorgeous?"

"Monroe," she answered.

Brent's grin widened even more and he bent over at the waist. "Nice to meet you, Monroe. Y'all don't sound like you're from around here."

"I'm not."

"So where're you from, sugar?" His eyes moved over her from head to toe, and something inside me tightened. I nearly stepped forward but caught myself in time. I wanted to shove him the hell away from her, and that was wrong. Monroe didn't belong to me. Shit, I barely knew the girl.

"I'm from New York City, and my name's not Sugar."

He snorted. "Your name might not be Sugar, but I bet you taste real sweet."

Monroe made a weird noise in the back of her throat, and I was surprised to see a hint of a smile on her face. "That's lame."

"Yeah, I guess it is." Brent chuckled, his eyes moving from Monroe back to me, and I saw the question there. Brent was a player. Big-time. I narrowed my eyes in warning. There was no way he was going there with this girl. Mrs. Blackwell would have my butt in a sling.

Brent was all about getting laid, which was pretty much the one thing most guys I knew thought about every single day. But him? Girls had been throwing themselves at him since he was twelve, and the ones who fell for his lame-ass lines deserved what they got.

But Monroe was different. And she didn't know him like I did.

"So, Monroe," Brent said carefully, cocking his head. "You want something to drink?"

She shook her head. "I'm driving."

"Right." Brent looked at me. "That means you're not." He grabbed a can from his back pocket and tossed it my way. "Come on," he said. "I've got a couple of guitars."

I popped the can open and took a long swig. The beer was lukewarm and not my favorite brand, but whatever, it was something to drink. Something to hold onto. Something to keep my hands busy.

"Are you sure that's a good idea?" Monroe said carefully, cocking her head to the side in a way that made a chunk of that dark tangled hair fall over her face.

I took another long drink and then wiped my mouth. "I'm not sure of anything right now."

For a moment, I thought I saw a small smile lift the corners of her mouth. I blinked and it was gone.

"Are you going to play for me?" she asked. Her eyes glistened; little sparks from the fire reflected in their depths.

"Yo, Nate."

The three of us turned as Chuck McDaniel strolled over with his girlfriend, Gina. I'd seen them earlier, at the festival, and wasn't surprised they had ended up out here. It's not like there was much else to do on Saturday night in Twin Oaks.

Gina's eyes narrowed on Monroe, her glossy lips pulled tight in a fake smile as she flexed her claws.

"Where's Rach?" she asked, though her eyes never quite made it to my face.

"Not here," I answered.

"I can see that." She snapped her gum and smiled. "And who are you exactly?" That was for Monroe.

"No one," Monroe answered, before tugging on my arm. "Are you going to play for me?"

"Come on, Everets. What's a party without some tunes?" Brent said.

"I don't know, man. I haven't picked up in forever." I took another long swig of beer and then crushed the can before shoving my hands into my front pockets. "I've probably lost my calluses, and knowing the way you've got your action rigged, my fingers will kill tomorrow."

"Pussy," Brent laughed. "Get your ass over here."

He was near the fire, and Monroe was two steps behind him. For a second, my eyes rested on her perfect round ass. On the way her hair swung down her back and how cute her feet looked with her green toes.

She turned, ignoring all the curious stares, and looked directly at me. For that one moment, it felt as if she was looking into my soul and she knew how badly I wanted to play.

"I want to hear you, Nate." Her voice was soft, so soft, like a whisper inside my head.

"Sugar, if you sweet-talked me up like that, I'd do anything you wanted," Brent said with a laugh as he bent closer to her. "Anything."

He turned to me and held out a beat-up Epiphone. Trevor's beat-up Epiphone.

"He'd want you to play, man." Gone was the laughter from Brent's face. "You need to play."

I stared at the guitar for so long that my eyes blurred, and when they began to sting, I knew this had been a bad idea. I should never have come here.

"No," I said, shoving my hands deeper into my pockets before I turned away from them. "It's not gonna happen."

I walked back toward Monroe's car and let the darkness slide over me.

# Chapter Eleven
## Monroe

I dreamt about Malcolm, which was something I hadn't done in months.

And sure, I should have seen it coming after my hospital visit—I didn't have to be a rocket scientist to know it would trigger all the bad things I'd been trying to forget—but still…I wasn't ready.

I wasn't ready to see his wavy blond hair touching tanned skin, or that one long piece that always fell over his eyebrow. I wasn't ready for the freckles along the bridge of his nose, so light they appeared to be sprinkles of cinnamon. Or his long lashes and the way they licked the tops of his cheeks when his eyes were closed. It hurt to see his dimple, the birthmark just under his collarbone, and the way it felt as if I was his entire world when he looked at me.

I wasn't ready for any of it, and that's why I woke up with screams in my throat, wiping sweat from my brow, my teeth clenched so tightly I was sure I'd ground them down another layer.

The ache in my heart felt like it was crushing me from the inside out, and for a few moments, I lay there shaking, sobbing quietly. I stuffed my fist into my mouth because it was late, or rather it was early in the morning, and I didn't want to wake Gram.

She didn't need to see me like this. Weak and broken. I knew she had hope. Hope that I'd come out of this summer ahead, maybe partway whole.

I also knew that her hope was false, but I didn't want to crush it.

The panic, though, was real, and I knew the drill, so I counted backward, starting at twenty. I had to do it more than once or twice even, and when I was finally calm—when the breath didn't catch in my chest and the pain had eased up a bit—sunlight was creeping into my room.

But it was hours before I left it.

• • •

"Monroe, have you talked to your parents today?"

We were on the porch, and I had just sat down beside Gram, sliding my feet beneath me as I curled into the white wicker chair. I stared down at my pink-and-white checker pajama shorts, noticing syrup had dripped from my morning pancakes onto the white T-shirt. I scraped it off with my finger, sucked it from the tip, and waited a few seconds to answer. Not because it was a trick question or anything, but because I hadn't called home and I didn't particularly *want* to call home, and I knew Gram was going to make me.

I focused on the honeysuckle climbing the trellis at the side of the house and the bees buzzing among them.

"I tried earlier but got Mom's voicemail, so I left a message." The white lie slipped out and I kept my gaze on the honeysuckle.

Gram's eyes rested on me for a few seconds, and I knew she wasn't fooled. "Well, if she hasn't returned your call in a few hours, try again. I know your mother doesn't always check her voicemail. You've been here over a week now. You need to talk to them. They'll worry."

"I emailed Mom yesterday."

"Bah," Gram said. "That email will be the death of society as we know it. It's not the same, Monroe."

"I know," I mumbled. "I'll call them tonight."

The truth of it was, talking to my parents was hard. So freaking hard. And right now, I liked not having anything hard in my day-to-day business. I hadn't realized how difficult it was for me to *breathe* in New York until I'd come to Louisiana.

"So," I said, chewing on my bottom lip, "Nate told me about Trevor."

I didn't volunteer that we had actually gone to the hospital—I figured that wasn't mine to share—but I was curious to see what Gram would say.

She settled back in her wicker chair, sipped her tea, and said,

"Good, that boy needs to talk to someone. What happened that night was an awful shame, but it's in the past." She glanced at me sharply. "And the past can't be undone, but we can surely do our best to move forward and learn from our mistakes."

My cheeks smarted at her meaning because I knew she was talking about me as well. I tucked a long piece of hair behind my ear and tried to think of something else besides the pathetic past I'd left in New York.

"Nathan's a good boy who made a bad decision, but he'll be fine. He's just hit a rough patch."

Huh. I thought of the scene I'd witnessed the night before, and in my mind, Nathan Everets had hit more than just a rough patch.

For a moment, the only sound I heard was the faraway drone of a plane crossing the sky above me. I glanced up and saw a trail of white cotton, but I couldn't see its source. The sun was too bright. Too hot.

It was going to be nasty today.

"He'll be here a lot over the next few weeks. His uncle told me that most of the work I've contracted will be done by Nathan."

I didn't say anything though my heart began to beat faster. Blowing out a long breath, I sank deeper into my chair, eyes still searching for the elusive plane, mostly because it gave me something to do.

Mostly because I could avoid Gram's eyes.

"I'm glad the two of you are getting on."

Oh God. My cheeks flushed. Getting on? That got my attention, and I glanced at her.

"He has a girlfriend, you know." What the hell was Gram up to?

"Does he now?"

I nodded. "Yes. Her name is Rachel."

Gram didn't have to say anything. I could tell from the way her mouth pinched at the corners as she took another sip of tea that she wasn't a fan of his girlfriend.

"How was the festival?" she asked instead, and I smiled. Gram was as good as me when it came to deflecting.

"It was…cute."

For a few moments, the silence of the morning enveloped us, broken only when Gram said something very unladylike and rose to her feet. She was late.

"Are you coming with me to service, Monroe?"

Shit.

"No?"

My answer came out more like a question, and for a moment, I was afraid she was going to make me go with her. I tugged on the edge of my T-shirt and exhaled, trying to stem the panic that I knew was there beneath my skin, just waiting to explode. I hadn't stepped inside a church since Malcolm's funeral, and my throat was already closing up at the thought of going.

I couldn't. Not yet. Maybe never.

"You go and I'll clean up the dishes from breakfast and call Mom and Dad."

Gram wiped an invisible crumb from her forearm, her silky white hair brushing her shoulders. She grabbed her teacup, turned toward the door, and spoke softly, her voice catching a bit and making me feel worse than I already did. "You're going to have to face all of this sooner than later, Monroe. All of it. And that means opening up to your parents and letting them in."

"I know, Gram," I whispered. "But not today…okay?"

Gram bent and kissed me as she walked by and then disappeared inside, leaving me alone with the bees and the honeysuckle.

Twenty minutes later, she pulled away in the Matlock, and I was washing up the few dishes we'd used for breakfast. My cell vibrated on the counter and I ignored it, drying the frying pan instead, but when it vibrated again, I tossed my towel aside, glaring at the phone.

I really didn't want to talk to my parents—not today. Not after the Malcolm dream when things were way too fresh in my mind, because I knew exactly what would happen. Dad would be polite, afraid that if he said the wrong thing it would trigger a relapse and send me back into the darkness. Back to before. And I got it. Before hadn't been pretty.

Before had been hell.

But what he didn't realize was that I didn't want polite. I didn't want the robot he'd become, because when I got the robot, it made me feel as if my dad was gone forever. And I'd already lost so much, the thought of never getting him back was more than I could handle right now.

And Mom would be all in my business, wanting to know every single boring thing I'd done. And then she would ask how I was feeling—if I was happy—which was stupid. We both knew I would never be happy again. Not really. So why ask?

And when I lied? When I told her that Gram and I were bonding over iced tea and kumbaya and that I was freaking A-okay? She would get emotional because she wanted to believe it so badly, and I would shut down because it was all a lie. And even though I knew my mom needed to believe things were going to be okay in order for her to survive, I hated that she could slide things under the rug and forget.

Or maybe I was jealous because I couldn't.

The cell phone blipped instead of buzzing and I grabbed it. Great. Now they were going to text me to death.

But it wasn't my parents sending me a text message.

It was Nate.


Thanks for last night. I owe you.


When had I given him my phone number? I chewed on my bottom lip and my heart sped up again, hitting a new level of insanity as I stared at his message. Crap.

What did he mean, he owed me? I rubbed my hand along my bare thigh, wondering what to say back to him, and I decided something casual was the way to go.

no probs.

Too much? Too little?
My phone bleeped almost instantly, and I jumped.

See you tomorrow.

If my heart was beating a mile a minute before, it kick-started into overdrive something fierce, and for a second, I was dizzy. Me. Monroe Blackwell. Dizzy over a stupid text message from a boy who not only had a girlfriend, but was as screwed up as I was.

I gave myself a mental smackdown and took a step back. Why was I getting so worked up over a few text messages? It's not as if they meant anything. The guy had a girlfriend. End of story.

I took a deep breath and typed a reply that I thought was appropriate.

okay.

And then winced. Lame.

I put the cell phone onto the table and watched it for way too long, but there was nothing. No more text messages. Only one longwinded voicemail from my parents telling me they were out for the day but would call later tonight.

With a groan, I headed upstairs to get dressed because I

knew Gram wouldn't let me stay in my pajamas all day, even if I begged her.

Just. Effing. Lovely.

# Chapter Twelve

# Nathan

I knew the moment Monroe arrived.

I'd just tossed the last empty water bottle into my bag after soaking my bandana and tying it around my head, and I knew that if I turned around, she'd be there. Don't ask me how. It's not like I'm psychic or anything. *I just knew.*

So I blew out a hot breath and turned around.

And there she was.

Her long hair was loose, kind of wild-looking, as if she hadn't brushed it. She wore cut-off jean shorts and a white Foo Fighters T-shirt that fit her like a T-shirt should fit a girl—tight in all the right spots. I had to give it to Monroe, the girl had good taste when it came to music. She tucked one long curl behind her ear and glanced behind me at the iron fence.

"You're done," she said.

I nodded. "Yeah. I started early. Figured it was a good idea 'cuz it's gonna be a hot one."

She cleared her throat and held out her hand. "Gram

thought you might want this. The lemonade is fresh. I squeezed it myself."

"Thanks," I murmured.

A slow blush crept into her cheeks as I stepped forward and took the tall glass filled with ice and lemonade. I liked the fact that I could make her blush. Our fingers touched briefly, and I liked the little zing that shot through me too.

I also liked the way her tongue darted out to take a swipe at her lips.

I followed the movement—what guy wouldn't? Monroe had a really nice mouth. Her cheeks reddened even more when she noticed, and I grinned.

"What are you doing this afternoon?" I asked, taking a long gulp of lemonade. My eyes didn't leave hers.

She shoved her hands into the back pockets of her jean shorts and shrugged. "I've got nothing exciting planned. Thought I might read a book or something."

I drained the glass and wiped my mouth. "You wanna go swimming instead?" Okay, I hadn't meant for that to slip out. "I owe you," I said in a rush as I waited for her to shoot me down.

"You owe me?"

"Yeah, for being my taxi Saturday night and for, well, everything else." I didn't mention the bush party or how lame I'd been, and I was glad when she didn't say anything about it.

Her eyes narrowed a bit. "Don't you have work to do?"

I shook my head. "Nope. I only had to finish this fence today.

Tomorrow I'm starting on the back porch at the main plantation house."

"Oh," she said softly, biting her mouth as her eyes fell away.

*"At least your mistake is still alive."*

Her words had rattled around in my head since Saturday night, and I knew that there was a lot more to Monroe Blackwell than a hot body and amazing eyes. And maybe I was stupid for wanting to get to know a girl who wasn't all that interested in me, but hey, I'd never been the guy to let something drop just because I thought my endgame wasn't achievable.

I wasn't even sure why I wanted to get to know her, except that sometimes when I looked into her eyes, *I* knew that *she* knew exactly what was going on inside me. And how crazy was that, considering I'd just met her?

"I know a really cool place, and it's not far from here, though…" my words faded to nothing.

Shit. My suspended license was going to bite me in the ass over and over again. Frustrated, I yanked off my bandana and balled it in my fist.

That got her attention, and once more, those pale green eyes focused on me. "What's wrong?"

"My car is still under house arrest, so it's not like I can actually take you anywhere." Pissed at myself, I offered her the glass back and shrugged. "Never mind. It was a stupid idea."

"Won't your girlfriend be mad if she found out you'd invited another girl to go hang at some watering hole? I mean, I'm not saying there's anything going on between us, because we both know that's not true, but still…"

*Oh, there's something going on. I just don't know what it is.*

"If I was the girlfriend of a guy who did that, I wouldn't be happy."

A shot of hope ran through me. So that was it. Her only thing was Rachel, and since Rachel and I had…

"I broke up with Rachel yesterday."

Sunday had sucked. Not surprising, considering the epic failure Saturday had been, but waking up to find a very naked Rachel in my bed had been the icing on the worst cake ever.

I can't lie. At first it had felt pretty damn good, but I guess that's because I'd been half asleep, and though I wouldn't admit it to anyone, in some far corner of my screwed-up head, I thought it was Monroe.

I'd been half asleep as Rachel kissed her way down my stomach and tugged on my boxers. I might have let her finish, but then she opened her mouth—and not in the way I'd been anticipating—and reality crashed in hard.

"Babe, I heard you went to the Peach Festival with some skank ho and then out to the bush party. Tell me it isn't true."

"Shit, stop," I said, coming fully awake.

"You're kidding, right?" She'd sat back, pissed and confused. "What the hell is wrong with you, Nate? On what planet do you turn down a blowjob?"

I pulled away and rolled out of bed, swearing as I tripped over her clothes and shoes.

What followed had been twenty minutes of listening to her scream and rant, and when she brought up Trevor and the accident, I blew her off and told her to leave. I especially didn't want to talk about that night with her.

I couldn't explain the feeling I got inside when I thought of the party and of Rachel and Trevor and his girlfriend, Bailey. Everything had been so great, and then in an instant, it was gone. All of it.

I was left with this dark, mean kind of feeling, and it made me hate myself more than I already did.

"You and Rachel…you guys broke up?" Monroe's soft voice brought me back from before, and it took a moment for me to focus.

I saw her clear eyes watching me warily. "Yeah."

"I'm sorry."

"Don't be. It was a long time coming." Longer even than the accident. The more I thought about it, I realized that Rachel and I hadn't been on the same page for a long, long time.

"Okay," she said.

I grabbed my bag and slung it over my shoulders before bending over and scooping up the paint can and brushes I'd used.

"Okay, what?"

"Okay, I'll give you a lift."

"A lift?" I took a few steps until I was close enough to smell that fresh scent that clung to her skin.

"Well, someone's gotta be your taxi, and since I don't have anything better to do, it may as well be me."

"So you're offering to drive me to Baker's Landing out of boredom."

A smile lifted the corners of her mouth, and I thought that her lips must feel incredibly soft. I thought that maybe it would be cool to find out just how soft they really were.

"Yes, Nathan. *Only* because I'm bored."

"Nate."

"What?"

"Call me Nate."

"Okay, *Nate*. But just so you know, I'm only giving you a ride. Nothing more."

"We're living in a freaking oven and you're not coming in?"

"I don't think I packed a bathing suit."

She started walking toward the house and I fell in beside her, liking the way she jumped when I leaned close and whispered, "Who says anything about wearing a bathing suit?"

She stopped so fast that I nearly ran her over. "I am *not* skinny-dipping with you."

Her cheeks were pink and hair stuck to the side of her neck. It was crazy that she could make me forget how shitty I felt about everything. Trevor. The accident. But I'd take it.

I'd play with it.

"Could be fun," I said with a laugh.

"For you maybe."

"What?" I said, watching her back as she walked away. "I know a lot of girls who'd love to get naked with me."

"I'm not one of them," she retorted.

I followed her, the grin still on my face.

She didn't say anything else until we hopped up the steps onto her Gram's porch. Here the shade was a bit cooler, but it was still nearing 100 degrees. I bet we could have tossed a few eggs onto the bottom step and the sun would have fried them in less than a minute.

"I'll be five minutes or so if you want to come inside?"

"Nah," I said. "I'm dirty. I'll just wait for you out here."

And then she was gone.

I stared down at my filthy work boots for a few seconds and then yanked them off, pulling out sandals from my bag. My T-shirt was pretty much drenched with sweat, and my hair was a crazy mess that stuck to my neck. Shit, maybe my dad was right and it was time for me to cut it the hell off.

I tore my shirt off and found an old baseball jersey that was wrinkled as all shit but at least it didn't smell.

I'd just slicked back my hair when the door slammed open and Monroe appeared with a beat-up green cooler and some towels.

"Gram made us lunch."

I was on my feet and took the cooler as Mrs. Blackwell followed her granddaughter onto the porch.

"Good afternoon, Nathan."

"Hey, Mrs. Blackwell. I hope you don't mind I'm heading out early, but it's hotter than a—" I thought better of cursing in front of Mrs. Blackwell and stopped myself just in time.

"That's fine, Nathan. Monroe says you've finished painting the fence around the family plot?"

"It's all done."

"Wonderful. And when are you starting on the main house?"

"Tomorrow, I think. My uncle needed to order some materials before we could start rebuilding posts that are rotted on the porch."

"Good." She paused and I shifted as she changed gears. "Where exactly are you taking my granddaughter?"

Her eyes were on me, focused and intense.

"I was thinking we could head out to Baker's Landing."

Baker's Landing was on my grandparents' land. It had the coldest, freshest, spring-fed water for swimming in the area, and on a day like today was the best place to cool off. I used to go out there a lot with Trevor and the guys, but so far this summer, I hadn't been once.

"There won't be any drinking."

"No, ma'am."

Mrs. Blackwell nodded. "All right, Monroe. But I expect you back for supper." With one last smile, she left us alone on the porch.

"You ready?" I said to Monroe as I headed down the steps. I got to the bottom before I realized that she hadn't followed.

"Anything wrong?" I asked carefully, wondering how I'd screwed this up already.

She played with soft pink straps that were tied behind her head and I realized she'd changed into a bathing suit when she'd been inside. "Will there be anybody else there?"

"I doubt it."

"I don't believe you."

I was quiet for a second, and then I got it.

"Rachel won't be there, if that's what you're worried about."

"Well, if she is, I'm leaving. I don't want to get in the middle of your crap."

"There is no middle, Monroe. There's no me and Rachel, not anymore. There's nothing."

She didn't answer but slipped into the driver's seat and fired up the old Crown Vic. For the first time in a long time, I realized I was looking forward to something and it was all because of the girl inside the car.

The girl with the gray/green eyes.

The girl with secrets and pain and something inside her that felt familiar. It was something that was close to what was buried inside my chest. Inside my head and heart.

And I thought that, for the first time since the accident, I didn't feel so alone.

And that was nice for a change.

# Chapter Thirteen
## Monroe

There wasn't a soul at Baker's Landing.

Not one person or dog or even a bird flying around. There was nothing except a hot breeze, beautiful oak trees, an inviting grassy knoll near the water, and the most picturesque pond I'd ever seen. Seriously. It looked like something out of a Nicholas Sparks movie, and I half expected a bunch of white swans to float by at any minute.

Or maybe Ryan Gosling rowing his boat like he'd done in *The Notebook*, looking so hot and yummy and sweaty…

*Kind of like Nate.*

I watched him as he walked toward the water, Gram's cooler in his hand, while the sun haloed him, giving him a surreal kind of look.

He moved like an athlete, long easy strides, and I could totally picture him on the football field, running plays and doing it really well. I thought that, if I lived around here, maybe I would go to his games. You know, if I liked football.

Which I didn't, so I don't even know why that thought popped into my head.

He paused on the edge of the bank, set the cooler on the ground, and peeled off his shirt.

My stomach did this weird dipping thing, but then why wouldn't it? The guy could be a model for the Abercrombie cargos he wore, and the fact that they hung so low I could see his boxers again didn't help.

It was almost worse than being naked, because it made a girl think of the unknown, and I shouldn't be thinking of the unknown.

*I shouldn't.*

Mostly because he was way out of my league—that's if I was interested, which I wasn't. I hadn't dated any guy in a long time—not since Malcolm died—and I knew that getting close to Nathan Everets wasn't a good idea.

So why was I thinking about it? Was it because, on some level, I knew he was unattainable? Was it because I knew Nate would never be interested in someone like me? A girl who was more damaged than he was? A girl with so much baggage she needed an extra set of luggage just to get her from day to day?

But if that was true, why had he brought me here? Was he just being nice? Or was he interested in someone who was different? Someone new?

Why did I care?

*God*, I groaned, *I'm such an idiot.*

I joined him and stared out at the water, shaking my head

when I spied a group of swans along the far side. Unbelievable. Totally Nicholas Sparks.

"You like it?"

He grinned down at me and I nodded, wishing he'd put his shirt back on or something. I dropped to the ground and dug through the cooler, handing him a ham sandwich when he did the same. We popped open a couple of cans of Coke and ate in silence, there beneath the biggest oak tree I'd ever seen.

For a few moments, the awkward silence between us made swallowing my food difficult. I couldn't think of anything to say, and the tension across my shoulders was starting to burn. I'm sure he thought I was an idiot.

I *was* an idiot. I should have just stayed home. Who was I kidding? I hadn't been alone with a boy in a very long time, especially a boy who made me feel things I wasn't used to feeling.

I shook my head. My therapist would be all over this shit.

"How long are you here for, Monroe?"

Thank God. A question I could answer.

I wiped a crumb from my lap. "'Til Labor Day weekend. My parents are coming from New York."

"Right. New York. I've never been, but it's on the list."

"The list?"

"Yep. The list of places I want to go. LA is at the top and New York is running a close second."

Huh.

"Trust me, it's overrated," I answered. I wished I didn't have to go back. It if wasn't for Kate and my parents, I'm not sure that I would.

"So do you go to a fancy school there in the Big Apple?"

I knew his eyes were focused on me, so I kept mine on the water, watching the swans slowly float in circles across the way.

"Yes," I said finally. Glen Hill Academy.

*I hate it there.*

"Why do you hate it there?"

Startled, I turned to Nate—which was the wrong thing to do, because he was staring at me with an expression that felt as if he could see right inside me. I swallowed hard and croaked, "Excuse me?"

His eyes never left mine. They held me trapped as surely as if he had some freaky kind of tracking device like on those old *Star Trek* movies I used to watch with my dad. The ones that pulled in objects and never let go.

"You said you hated it there. I just wondered why."

Shit. Had I said that out loud? What was wrong with me?

"It reminds me too much of someone," I blurted, my heart picking up steam and banging inside my chest wall like a demented drummer. What the hell kind of power did this guy have?

Some weird expression crossed his face, and then he spoke softly. "I'm sorry."

"Yeah, well don't be." I shrugged. "It's not a big deal."

Except it was. It was a very big deal. And it was a big deal that wasn't going to go away, no matter how much I pretended it would.

It was the big deal that had broken me.

"Let's go in," Nate said abruptly, jumping to his feet and holding out his hand for me.

I glanced at the water again and then back up to him.

"You're not afraid of the swans, are you?" he challenged.

"No," I answered, ignoring his hand as I got up. A shiver rolled over me, which was odd considering it was so darn hot. "Is the water clean?"

He'd chucked his sandals and had his hands on the waistband of his shorts. My mouth went dry, and some stupid lump decided to clog my throat as I watched him begin to tug them down over his hips.

"What are you doing?" I squealed. I thought of his teasing earlier, and my alarm ramped up to about one million. There was no way I was gonna skinny-dip with Nathan Everets. No effing way.

His grin was as annoying as ever. "I don't have a bathing suit with me, so I'm gonna go in with my boxers." He paused, his hands tucked *inside* his boxers. "Unless you want me to—"

"No, boxers are fine." I tried not to stare when he stepped out of his shorts, but it was hard. The guy was ripped. He was ripped and hot and sexy and he was standing a foot away in a pair of black athletic boxers that didn't hide anything. And holy hell but Nathan Everets had a lot to hide.

I swallowed hard and turned away, easing out a long breath, when I heard a splash and knew he was in the water.

"Damn, but this feels great. Get your ass in here, Blackwell!"

I turned and spied him halfway across the pond, floating on his back for a few seconds before he whooped and disappeared beneath the surface once more.

The sun made the surface of the water shimmer like diamonds, and seconds later, his head popped up closer to shore—closer to me. He grinned and I couldn't help but do the same as I watched him. He was like a little kid, and there was something adorable about that.

"Come on. Get your clothes off or I'll come out and get you."

Alarmed, I took a step back. "I told you I wasn't sure if I was going in or not." I wasn't normally shy or anything, but the thought of Nate seeing me in my bikini made me nervous. Or excited. Or both.

But the thought of being so close to him when we were practically naked was way worse. *That* made me feel all kinds of things I hadn't felt since…

Heck, who was I kidding? I hadn't felt any of those things before. Not even back then. And it had been so long since I'd had any kind of fun. Since I'd *felt* like having any kind of fun that, for a moment, I don't even think I realized what it was I was feeling.

Anticipation.

"Okay, I'm coming to get you."

My head whipped up and I squealed, hands on my shorts. "No, I'm coming in."

But he didn't listen, and I'd barely gotten out of my clothes when he was there, inches from me. His tall body, wet and shiny and incredible.

My eyes dropped.

His boxers were wet and…

My breath caught as I slowly slid my eyes back up over all that skin. Over the razor-thin line of hair that disappeared beneath his boxers. Over the washboard stomach and rippled abs. Higher to the tattoo on his shoulder and arm that said danger. And sex. And danger.

*Sex.*

Up past his defined chest and broad shoulders.

Until I met eyes that jump-started something in me that was foreign. Something that was hot and exotic and scary.

Something that was so incredibly alive, it made me weak. I'd been half dead for so long, the sensation was almost overwhelming, and I bit my lip as tears stung the corners of my eyes.

Quickly I glanced away, ashamed at my reaction and feeling like a total dork. What was I doing here? I couldn't play this game with Nate because I had no idea how to play it. I'd been locked in a cocoon of pain for so long that I didn't even know how to communicate and act normal with a regular boy, let alone someone like Nathan Everets—a guy who was so far above me I wasn't sure I'd ever be able to reach him.

But the way he looked at me sometimes…

Suddenly aware of how revealing my pink bikini was, I crossed my arms over my chest and shivered.

My eyes squeezed shut, and I wished I was home with Gram, curled up on the front porch with a book I pretended to read while she flipped through her gardening magazines.

"Hey," Nate said, a touch of rasp in his voice, and I thought that maybe a tremor rippled just beneath. "Are you all right?"

I nodded, afraid to say anything because I didn't trust that I wouldn't make a complete ass out of myself.

"Good."

And then two strong arms were around my waist and a shriek fell out of me—one that would have made my mother proud—as Nate lifted me over his shoulder and carried me to the edge.

I didn't get a chance to say anything because at the moment, my brain was focused on how hard he felt. There were no soft curves—there was no soft anything. He was all hard, lean, and muscled lines, and his skin burned into mine.

And God, he smelled so good.

I shook my head, suddenly aware that my butt was near his face and that his hand was on the small of my back, holding me in place. When I finally got my shit together and opened my mouth to say something, it was too late.

There was the feeling of air on my exposed skin. Sun in my eyes. And then there was the shock of cold water.

I went deep and began to kick my legs, grateful for the silence that fell over me and the darkness in which I could hide, however briefly. My legs kicked and kicked, my arms joining in, and when I finally surfaced and cleared the water from my eyes, I was surprised to see that I'd swum halfway across the large pond.

I glanced down. Good. Bikini still in place, nothing exposed that shouldn't be.

The swans protested and took off, their large graceful bodies slicing through the air as they landed on the soft grassy bank, honking their annoyance.

Treading water, I turned around and I think I might have yelped when I spied Nate so close to me, his head above water as he watched me intently.

I wished he didn't make me feel so nervous. I didn't like nervous. It meant that I wasn't in control, and ever since that awful night, the one I don't like to talk about or remember, I was all about being in control.

"Feels good," he said softly. It wasn't a question.

I nodded, my eyes not leaving his as he floated closer. Wet, his hair clung to his neck and disappeared into the water, while a slow grin swept across his mouth.

I began to move backward. I couldn't touch the bottom where we were, and I had no idea how long I could tread water before I'd begin to tire.

I moved back maybe ten feet and he kept pace, his eyes still on mine. Still making me nervous.

"What are you doing?" I said roughly, eyeing the bank but thinking the swans wouldn't be happy if I hauled my butt out onto their territory. Did swans attack people? Should I chance it?

"What do you think I'm doing?" he asked.

I thrust my chin up and made a face. "I don't know. That's why I asked."

I refused to keep playing whatever game this was, so I continued to tread water, and even when he floated so close I could see the drops that clung to his eyelashes, I refused to budge. I wasn't used to these kinds of games.

"What do you want me to do?" he asked.

I said nothing because I had no idea what to say, so I shrugged, which was kind of hard to do while treading water.

"I've been thinking about kissing you since yesterday."

Holy. Hell.

"Really," I managed to say, glad to hear the tinge of sarcasm I was going for was present.

"Yes." His finger grazed my thigh, and I swear my heart was going to beat out of my chest. "Really."

He rose up in the water an inch or so, making me suddenly aware that even though I was treading water, he was tall enough to stand.

"Well, what are you waiting for?"

Holy shit. Did that just come out of my mouth? Was I crazy?

Uh. Stupid question. I'd been seeing a therapist for over a

year and I'd slit my wrist. Sure, it had been a lame, halfhearted attempt, but still…I was pretty sure that passed as freaking crazy in anyone's book.

A heartbeat passed.

And then another.

His dark eyes glittered. His hands rolled over my shoulders, and he pulled me so close that I felt the heat from his skin on mine. It seared through the cool water, and I felt it like a handprint as his fingers moved down my thigh, coaxing my legs up until I wrapped them around his waist in such a way that it made all kinds of hot, needful things erupt inside me.

I couldn't breathe. I couldn't think.

I was awash in sensations and feelings, and for once, I didn't turn them off. I let them roll over me. I let them roll *into* me. Because they felt so damn good. Because they made me feel alive, and for once, I was just going to let them be.

I wanted to feel again. Was that so wrong?

And when his mouth rested near my ear, my hands slowly crept up until I clung to his shoulders like a child afraid to fall.

"I was waiting for this," he said.

My eyes squeezed shut, and I loved the feel of his hard body against me. He was real. Solid. *Alive.*

I might have groaned or made some other equally embarrassing noise, when I inhaled sharply, hot fires burning everywhere inside me as his hand moved to my butt and he held me even tighter against him. It had been so long since I'd let anyone touch me, let alone hold me like this. Like we were already a part of each other.

"Are you done waiting?"

"Yeah," he said throatily. "I am.

## Chapter Fourteen

# Nathan

I had never wanted to kiss a girl as badly as I wanted to kiss Monroe Blackwell. Never.

Not even that first time, when I'd pressed myself against Rachel and she'd opened her shirt so that I could see her boobs. I knew I was gonna get a hell of a lot more than a kiss from Rachel, but even then, I didn't feel like I did right now.

Like I was coming apart. Like if I didn't hold Monroe as close to me as I could, I would explode.

I was hot and tight and hard. And I knew that if she moved an inch or so lower, she would know just how hard I was. It wasn't like I could hide it.

She made this noise, this almost painful-sounding noise, and my hands clutched at her, holding her in place, because suddenly I was afraid I was gonna lose it big-time. I'd gone from zero to freaking one hundred in less than a minute, and I didn't know if I could control the shit that was going on inside me.

I was so afraid of scaring her off that I nearly let her go. I nearly let her float away from me, because as much as she was into this right now, I knew that I needed to take things slow with her. I thought of her eyes. Of the secrets they held. I thought of the pain I'd glimpsed, and something inside me twisted.

What was I doing? I was no good for her. Hell, with the crap going on in my life, I wasn't good for anybody.

"Are you done waiting?" she said.

I blinked, my body tightening even more if that was possible. *No.*

Then she moved a bit—we were skin on skin. She made that sound again, and I was done.

"Yes," I said, barely able to answer. "I am."

I'd kiss her. And maybe it would suck. Maybe all this other stuff didn't mean shit when it came to actual kissing.

Her pupils were huge, her long hair slicked against her shoulders, and her mouth was shiny and open. She shuddered against me as I bent forward and gathered her even closer.

I felt her legs tighten around my waist, and I think I stopped breathing until my mouth slid over hers and she exhaled into me.

At first, she was hesitant, her lips trembling a little beneath mine, but then her fingers dug into my shoulders and she opened up, her tongue sliding into my mouth and driving me crazy. She was warm and soft and smooth beneath my fingers, and her mouth was as amazing as I had imagined.

No, that was wrong, because everything was way better than

I'd imagined. The way she felt. The way she tasted. Those little noises she kept making.

We kissed for a long time. Long enough for me to know that if I didn't stop things, I was gonna embarrass myself in ways a guy should never do with a girl he liked.

Carefully, I pulled away, though her legs were still wrapped around my waist as if they belonged there.

We were both breathing pretty heavy, and for a few long seconds, I stared down into the most amazing eyes I'd ever seen, and the cool thing was, there were no shadows. No pain. No sadness.

There was just Monroe.

"Hey," I managed to say.

She glanced away, but not before I saw the ghost of a smile. "Is that your lame attempt to get me naked?"

"Did it work?" I answered, letting her float away.

She splashed me. "Do I look naked?"

"Not yet."

She splashed me again, this time filling the air with laughter. "I don't know why you're trying, Nate. I don't do stuff like that. Not with boys like you."

"Hey," I said with a grin. "Should I feel insulted? What do you mean, boys like me?"

"You know," she said softly. "Boys who can make a girl forget."

"What is it that you want to forget?" I asked, breath held as I waited for her to answer.

Her eyes bored into mine and something flashed inside them. "I'll never tell," she answered softly.

She'd drifted far enough away for my body to cool down a bit, and I moved after her, treading water to keep my distance. I had the feeling that Monroe needed some space. Maybe I did too.

So for a few moments, we floated and said nothing. When she eventually made her way to the other side of the bank, I watched her walk out and then followed her, flopping down beside her on the large blue-and-white checker blanket her Gram had given us.

It didn't take long for the sun to dry the water on our skin, and when she rolled over and began to slap on sunscreen lotion, I had to look away. I mean, a guy could only take so much, and the little bikini she wore didn't hide the fact that every inch of her was beautiful.

"You want some?" she asked.

"Nah." I shook my head. Because I was outside all the time, my skin was tanned. I was good.

She slipped on a pair of sunglasses and offered me another Coke. It was cold and felt good going down.

"How come you won't play guitar?" she asked suddenly, not looking at me but out over the water.

I followed her gaze but didn't answer right away. I had to give it to Monroe—she sure as hell knew how to kill the mood.

"Why do you care?"

She shrugged. "I don't really. I'm just curious. It seems as if music is a huge part of your life and you've kind of shut it down."

I scowled. Huh.

Couldn't argue with that logic.

"I'm sorry," she said. "I didn't mean to make you angry."

"I'm not angry."

She turned her head and tipped her glasses down her nose. "Yeah, you are, Nate."

Somewhere overhead, a plane crossed the sky, and off in the distance, I heard a chainsaw echo. I fell back, throwing my arms over my eyes for shade.

"Playing reminds me of Trevor. It reminds me of all the things he can't do. The things he might never do again, and that's all on me." I had to pause because the emotion was there, burrowed in my chest, and I didn't want it to get hold of me. Not here. Not with Monroe.

"All of it. That night. It all went south, and Trevor's dad is right. It's my fault."

"But there were four of you there that night, right?"

I didn't answer.

"So how can his father think it's your fault? Isn't Trevor a big boy? Used to making his own decisions?"

"You don't get it." I sprang forward and wrapped my arms around my knees. "I was the one who drove that night. I made that call. Did something stupid and irresponsible, and now he's in a coma."

Monroe rolled over onto her stomach and rested her head on her arms. "Don't you think it could have been any one of you guys driving?"

I shook my head. "Not that night. It was my turn." The burn in my gut made my voice shake a little, but I couldn't help it. "We always did that when it came time to party. We took turns, and that night it was mine. It was mine and I screwed up, and nothing will ever be the same again. If I could go back in time and change it, I would, but I can't and now there's no more music. I just don't…feel the music anymore."

"I think—"

She didn't have a chance to finish because I cut her off. "Don't think, Monroe." I rolled over and grabbed the sunscreen. "I don't want to talk about it."

"What are you doing?" she angled her head back, her pale eyes wary as I grinned at her.

"Do you want your skin to burn?"

She was too late to answer, and I squirted coconut-scented lotion near the small of her back. Slowly I rubbed it upward, enjoying the view and liking that she was quiet. God, her skin was soft. And the color? It was creamy, white, like the alabaster carvings my grandfather loved.

My fingers looked dark against her, and something about the way they looked and felt made me tight again. I was starting to lose focus—my hands began to travel back down to where they started, and that wasn't a good idea.

When I was done, I tossed the tube and slid back down beside her.

I'm not sure how long we lay there, so close that it felt as if we were together, but the silence between us made it feel as if she was across the lake.

"Still trying to get me naked?" she said abruptly, and I grinned. I was glad she had made the effort to lighten whatever this was between us. Light was good. Light made things bearable.

"Nope."

"Huh."

I glanced her way and found those pale eyes on me, and for a moment, I forgot what I was going to say. Her smile widened and she shot her elbow out, hitting me in the arm.

"You sound like you don't believe me."

She shook her head. "That's because I don't. I know what you guys are like."

"You guys?" I guess I should have been insulted, but I wasn't.

"Yeah," she said softly. "Rocker guys. They're always trying to get into some girl's pants."

Slowly, I pushed myself up until I kneeled beside her, and then I leaned forward, pushing away a long chunk of hair so I could whisper near her ear.

"You're not just any girl, and Mrs. Blackwell would skin my ass if I pulled any kind of shit on you."

"That's right," she said, and I heard a quiver in her voice. "Don't forget it. Gram is fierce."

"That doesn't mean I won't kiss you again."

I smiled and ran my fingers over her shoulders, liking the way she trembled beneath them.

There was silence. For a heartbeat. Maybe two.

"I might let you kiss me again." She shrugged and rolled over so that she was up on her knees as well. Her skin was pink and it wasn't from the sun. I was pretty sure it was all about the heat between us.

"You'll *let* me?" I wasn't teasing anymore. Mostly because my eyes dropped to her mouth and that damn pink tongue of hers was resting between her teeth. Her chest rose and fell rapidly, in tandem with the heavy beats of my heart.

When her eyes fell to my mouth, I might have groaned. Pussy move, but man, she really tugged at all kinds of shit inside me.

"When you play your guitar," she paused and exhaled. "When you play just for me, Nate. I'll let you kiss me again."

She was up on her feet in a flash, a blur of pink bikini, pale skin, and dark hair. The sun blinded me when I glanced up, and for a few seconds, all I saw was a shadow with a ring of gold.

And then she was gone.

# Chapter Fifteen

# Monroe

I didn't see Nate for the rest of the week and not because he wasn't around. He'd shown up Tuesday morning with his uncle, and they started working on the back porch up at the main plantation house.

It was a pretty big project, and the two of them worked from early in the morning until dinnertime. He texted me a few times, but after two days, he stopped. I guess he wasn't impressed with my one word answers.

**Nate:** What cha doin?
**Me:** nothing
**Nate:** wanna hang later
**Me:** No
**Nate:** is something wrong
**Me:** No

Except that there was. Nathan Everets confused me. The feelings he made me feel confused me. And every time I thought about being with him, I got all nervous and anxious, and I just didn't do any of that real well.

It might have been immature of me, but my reaction to our afternoon at the pond was to stay away, and even I didn't understand it. And I sure didn't have enough experience with boys to know what to do about it.

So I avoided him.

I didn't go anywhere near the main plantation house, and when Gram suggested I take Nate some lemonade, I told her that I was pretty sure he had a supply of his own drinks.

Gram had given me her signature look—the one that made most people cave and just do whatever it was that she wanted done. But I didn't fall for it.

I was pulling away, and Gram knew it. It's what I did. But for now, she let it go, smart enough to know that if she pushed harder, I would disappear. I'd climb back into that dark hole I'd barely made it out of.

I knew Gram wanted to help me, and I'm pretty sure she thought she could help Nathan too. But he made me nervous. He made me feel. And I needed time for those things.

Only we don't always get what we want.

Friday morning came with a blast of heat, the promise of rain, and no Nate. Something had come up, and he and his uncle had gone to another job site. I heard Gram's one-sided conversation while picking at my bowl of Lucky Charms. I'd already eaten all the green marshmallows and was on to the pink ones.

She hung up and turned to me, her soft white hair already set, the curls perfect, but in this heat, they wouldn't be for long.

"Do you want to come shopping with me, Monroe?"

I pushed my bowl away, feeling that restlessness inside expand and tighten up. "Where?"

"Just to town. I want to go to market before the weather turns."

I shrugged. "Sure." It's not like I had anything better to do.

After a quick shower, I pulled on a pair of faded jean shorts and a white tank top and slipped my feet into a pair of old flip-flops before pulling my damp hair into a loose side pony.

I'm not sure what made me do it, but I grabbed some gloss from Gram's bathroom for my lips and ran her mascara brush over my eyelashes. For a few moments, I stared at the reflection in the mirror. I knew I would never be as tanned as the girls I'd met here, but my cheeks weren't as pale as they used to be and my eyes...

I glanced away, scrubbing at the corners of my eyes. I almost looked *not* sad. I almost looked normal. Pretty even.

"What do you care," I muttered before running out to meet Gram.

A half an hour later, she pulled up to the old fairgrounds. There were several smaller buildings scattered around an area as big as a football field. But the largest one was where all the local farmers gathered every Friday to sell their fresh fruit, produce, and pretty much anything else you wanted.

That's the thing about these southern folks. They sure liked to buy and sell, and they sure liked to gossip.

I followed Gram inside where the air was cooler in the shade, and it took a few seconds for my eyes to adjust. The building was filled with all sorts of vendors and—I sniffed—probably livestock somewhere.

"I'm going to have a look at the produce, Monroe. Can you take this bag and grab some peaches and whatever else you want?" She nodded to the aisle across from me and handed me some cash.

I headed down the aisle, sidestepping more than a few people who weren't paying attention. One lady backed into me, her elbow hitting me in the chest, and she turned around as if it was my fault.

"Watch where you're going," she said in a huff.

Rolling my eyes, I moved past her, searching for the booth that sold peaches. I figured the sooner I found what Gram wanted, the sooner we could head back to the plantation and I could get ready for an exciting afternoon of nothing.

I'd just spotted the peaches when someone grabbed my arm.

"Hey, Monroe, right?"

It was Brent. Nate's buddy.

His voice was as warm as his eyes, and I nodded, smiling. "Hey."

He waved to someone behind me, his smile still in place. "Seen Nate lately?"

"No, I haven't seen him since Monday."

He frowned. "I thought he was working out at your grandmother's."

"He is, but I…we just…" God, I sounded like an idiot,

and the longer I stumbled over my words, the wider Brent's smile became.

"You guys have a fight?"

"What? No." I took a moment. Gathered my thoughts. "We're not even friends really, so…"

Brent snorted and leaned close. "Yeah. Okay."

"What are you doing here?" I asked, changing the subject. Deflecting like I always did.

He held up a few bags. "Running errands for my mom. You?"

"Same. I need some peaches for my gram."

I moved toward the booth, aware that Brent followed, and when I paid for the peaches, he grabbed my bag. "I'll help you with this."

"You don't have to."

"I know I don't have to, Sugar, but us good old southern boys are all about helping when we can."

I wasn't sure what to say. It's not as if I had a lot of practice making small talk with boys. In fact, I had zero practice.

"What do you want?" I asked abruptly, coming to a full stop and wincing because I knew I sounded like a bitch. "Look, I'm sorry, I didn't mean to sound so…I just…" I sighed. "I don't know what I mean."

And I didn't. What was wrong with me?

"Don't worry about it." He laughed. "I'm just trying to figure you out. You're different from most girls around here."

"There's not much to figure out," I retorted. Different? What the hell did that mean?

We reached the entrance, and I felt the heat from outside slide across my skin. I spotted Gram across the way, chatting with a few ladies, her arms heavy with vegetables.

"Look," Brent said. "Nate is one of my best buddies, and right now he's going through some shit. Some really bad shit."

"I know." I moved so that the large woman who'd nearly run me over earlier could pass.

"He told you about what happened?"

"Yeah."

"Shit."

"Yeah."

"Look, the thing is, none of us knows where his head is at. He broke up with Rachel. He's not talking to any of us, and the guy won't even pick up his guitar. That's just wrong. God, it's wrong on so many levels. I heard what happened at the hospital. I heard that Mr. Lewis rode his ass hard."

"It wasn't pretty."

"You were there?" He seemed surprised.

"Yeah."

"Well, maybe you can…" Brent seemed at a loss and hunched his shoulders, kicking the ground with his shoes.

"I can what?"

"Maybe you can help him. He needs something, you know? Something good right now, because as long as Trevor's in the hospital, Nate is stuck in all the shit that happened that night, and honestly? It could have been any one of us behind the wheel. Shit happens. Mistakes happen."

"Were you there?" I asked, more than a little curious.

Brent handed me my bag, his eyes on the ground.

"Yeah. I was there that night. I got there late. Had a fight with the girl I'd been dating, so I was stone sober. I offered to drive them home before I got into it but…"

"But what?"

He looked up and I saw moisture in his eyes. Brent exhaled and shrugged, wiping at the corners of his eyes. "Trevor said no. He told me that Nate was good, and I believed him. I guess Nathan's not the only one who screwed up that night. I should have checked, but I didn't. I knew those guys were partying hard, but they were always good about the driving thing. They took turns. We all did." He sighed. "I was pissed and all I wanted to do was crack open my bottle of Jack and hopefully get laid."

Brent swore and ran his hands across his chin, his eyes on me. "I wish we could go back, you know? Back to before that night when everything was good. Because nothing is the same, and it sucks."

No shit.

"Hi, Mrs. Blackwell." He waved to Gram as I took a step forward, but his hand stopped me. "What are you doing tonight?"

Warily, I studied him for a moment, wondering what his angle was. "Nothing. Why?"

"A bunch of us jam at the Coffee House every other Friday. It's a small place in town. We do acoustic stuff. Lots of singing. Playing. It's a good time. You should come."

I wasn't sure what was going on. Was Brent asking me out?

"Unless you want to stay home with your grandma and watch *Jeopardy!*," he continued. "'Cause I'm sure that will be a good time too."

And that was pretty much what the evening held for me. Not that I didn't like being with Gram, but there was only so much *Jeopardy!* I could take.

Surprisingly, I kinda wanted to go, except…

"I don't really know anyone."

He arched an eyebrow. "You know Nathan. Tell him to come, and while you're at it, tell him to bring his guitar."

I started to protest, but Brent cut me off.

"He needs this, Monroe. It can't hurt to ask." He paused and smiled so sweetly at me that I was pretty sure it was something he'd done a hundred times before. "Please?"

Gram was at the car by now, loading her bags into the trunk. "What time?"

"Around nine." Brent grinned and I saw the relief in his eyes, but I had to set him straight. I knew a little bit about the process of healing—or not healing—and nothing was easy.

"He'll probably say no."

"Probably. Though I think he'll have a hard time saying no to you."

"Really," I said dryly.

"I know *I* would." He grinned. "*Sugar.*"

The guy had enough charm to light up an entire city block in New York, and I couldn't help but smile. "I can't promise, but I'll try."

"Cool," he said. "I'll save you guys a seat."

# Chapter Sixteen

# Nathan

When my cell pinged, I almost didn't answer it.

Rachel had been texting me for days now. She was incessant, and I knew that she wouldn't stop because she was real stubborn. Always had been. I used to like that about her.

But right now, she couldn't get that I wasn't into her anymore. She thought that us breaking up was about the accident, but she was wrong.

The events of that night were like a cancer that was growing and wouldn't stop. But the seeds of that cancer had started a long time ago, and she was part of it. I was outgrowing the endless parties and good times—Trevor and I both were. Music had pretty much become everything to us, and it was hard to write really good songs when you were wasted.

And wasted is what she was all about these days.

It hadn't always been that way. Rachel used to make me laugh. She used to have this way of making everything light and easy. We used to hang at Trevor's and play guitar and write songs and she'd listen to us, this big grin on her face because she really dug what we were doing.

God, she'd walk into a room and most every guy's head would swivel around, and I was proud that she was my girl. But then something changed, and I don't really know what it was. Maybe I just outgrew what we had. Maybe I outgrew our friendship, or maybe it was Rachel.

Bottom line was that I stopped thinking of Rachel as someone I loved a long time ago. I mean, I loved her, but not in the way a guy should love his girlfriend.

Music was my thing, and it had kind of taken over. It was mine and Trevor's. It was all we lived for. And he knew how I felt about Rachel, about how I was going to break up with her. I'd planned on doing it that night, but then everything had gone to shit.

So I'd let it fester for three more months, and though I had finally stepped up and cut her out, the cancer was still spreading, and I didn't know how to stop it.

I didn't know how to end it because the cancer was connected. It was connected to me and Trevor, and if it took my best friend whole, I was pretty damn sure it would take me too.

The cell pinged again and I stared at it, not moving. We'd finished dinner and my mom had just cleared the plates. I heard her and Dad in the kitchen, talking softly, murmuring to each other. They were worried. Worried about me.

I didn't deserve their worry or my mom's sad looks or the way she tried to smile though her pain.

"Are you going to answer that?" Dad's voice jerked me from wherever the hell my mind was at, and I glanced over to him.

I shrugged. "Doubt it. It's probably Rachel again."

I'd migrated to the family room, and he slid into the leather chair across from me. The big screen was on, the Texas Rangers were pounding the crap out of the Dodgers, but there was no sound. There was only the shit inside my head.

Dad leaned forward. "You guys broke up?"

"Yeah."

"You have a fight?"

I looked at him as if he'd lost his mind, and he held his hands up.

"Just asking."

I shook my head. "We didn't have a fight. We just…we just don't fit anymore."

"It happens."

"Yeah."

He cleared his throat. "I ran into Mike Lewis today."

That had me sitting up. "Is Trevor okay?"

"He's the same." My dad blew out a long breath. "Mike told me you were there last Saturday."

My eyes slid away. "I needed to see him, Dad."

"I know." My dad got up and walked over until his knee was touching mine. He bent forward, clasped my shoulders in the way that guys do, and I hated that all the pain inside me was bubbling, just there, just underneath my skin like invisible scars.

"They hate me for what I did."

He ran his fingers across the top of my head, just like he used to do when I was little, and a big lump clogged my throat.

"It's not hate," he said roughly. "It's…you have to understand the place that Mike and Brenda are living in is dark. Mike's taking it out on you because he has no one else to hit. Right now, you're it. You're the face he sees when he's in pain, but he'll come around."

"I should be lying in that bed, not Trevor."

"No." His voice was sharp. Sharp and rough. "Don't you ever say that again."

"It's the truth."

Something snapped in my dad. His eyes got all weird and his mouth was tight as he glared at me.

"I will tell you right now that I don't want to hear that kind of crap coming out of your mouth. Understand? What happened is in the past. There's nothing you can do to change what you did that night. It's done. Finished. Do you understand?"

But he didn't get it. I wasn't so sure his answers were the right ones.

"It's not over. Don't you get that? No matter how much you all want it to be over." My voice was loud, and I shifted away from him. "It's all I can think about. It's in my head every single day. If Trevor…" I had to stop for a second. "If Trevor doesn't make it…" but I didn't have the balls to finish my thought. I couldn't say the words out loud, so I left them hanging.

"I know it's hard, Nathan, but shutting yourself out and taking a vacation from life isn't the answer either."

"You don't get it," I replied. "It's so much more than just a mistake. A mistake is putting milk in your coffee instead of cream, or calling the wrong play in a game."

"I'm not minimizing what you did, Nathan. I would never do that. *You made a mistake.* You. All on your own, and it was one with tragic consequences. But you're going to have to live with them. You're going to have to deal with them." His voice broke, and I felt the heat of tears stinging my eyes. "No one is perfect. Remember that."

That was me all right. Far from freaking perfect.

"Yeah, well, my bad decision just might kill my best friend or leave him damaged for good. He'll hate me forever."

"Maybe." My dad pushed away. "Maybe not. But whatever happens, we'll deal with it. Your mom and I are here for you. I hope you know that."

"You guys must be so ashamed." We'd never really talked about this stuff before. After that night, when they'd come for me in the hospital, my mom had talked about everything except what had happened. And my father? He'd been real quiet. Scared.

"I'm not ashamed of you, Nathan. Don't ever think that." He shoved his hands into his pockets. "I wish that you didn't have to deal with any of this. I wish that Trevor was good and healthy and that you guys were off with the band playing a show tonight."

"That's not gonna happen," I muttered.

"No, it's not, and I'm sorry it didn't turn out that way. But I believe that the events of that night also set into motion the things that will define you. The things that will make you into the man I know you can be."

My cell pinged, but this time it was a call.

"You should answer that," he said quietly.

When he was gone, I glanced down, jerking forward when I saw who it was. Monroe.

I clenched my jaw as a wave of anger rolled over me. After Sunday, I'd thought...hell, I don't know what I had thought. But I sure didn't think she'd act as if I didn't exist. Maybe she had figured out what everyone else already knew. That I was bad news.

The phone pinged for several more seconds and then stopped. I waited for a few minutes and then checked my voicemail, but there was nothing.

Tossing it, I sank back into the sofa, rested my head, and gazed up at the ceiling. I kept clenching and unclenching my hands, hating the heaviness inside me. But I had no idea how to lighten the load, and despite what my dad said, I wasn't so sure I deserved it.

I'm not sure how long I was there, alone with all that darkness. It could have been minutes, but judging by the gloom outside, I was guessing it had been at least an hour. My mom poked her head in, a smile on her face.

"There's a girl here for you, Nathan."

"Yeah?" I angled my head so that I could look at her. "Tell me it's not Rachel." My mom wasn't exactly a fan of Rachel. Hadn't been ever since tenth grade when she'd come home from work early and found Rachel and me in bed. Naked and in the middle of getting busy.

Even so, at this point I was willing to bet Mom would let us go at it wherever the hell we wanted to, if that would make me happy. She just wanted to see me smile again.

"It's not Rachel. It's a really pretty girl with long dark hair. She says her name is Monroe and that you were expecting her." She paused, her forehead wrinkling. "Who is she?"

Huh.

"Mrs. Blackwell's granddaughter." I saw the look in my mom's eyes. "Hey, don't get all excited. First off, she's only here for the summer, and secondly, we're not exactly friends."

I scowled. She'd made it more than clear that I was nothing.

"Tell her I'm not home." I added.

"I can't." Mom pushed back her long, blond hair and walked over to me, nudging my knee with hers as she rolled back on her feet. "She knows you're here. If you want to blow her off, you're going to have to do that yourself."

"Awesome," I said, jumping up to my feet.

My mom was on the small side, about Monroe's height, and she had to stretch to reach me. She kissed my cheeks and whispered, "You're welcome."

I watched her leave through the patio doors that led to the back garden. My dad was out there, and I guessed she was trying to give me some space to deal with the "pretty girl" who'd come to see me.

Did I want to see Monroe? Did I have a choice?

"Screw it," I muttered and headed toward the front door.

I smelled that summer scent that was all Monroe before I hit the foyer, and for a second, I let it wash over me.

"Pussy," I said under my breath.

So she smelled good. She was still the prickliest, most complicated girl I'd ever met, and just because kissing her had pretty much been the highlight of my pathetic summer, it wasn't like it had meant anything to her. She'd blown me off.

But I was curious as to why she had come to see me, and I guess it was that curiosity that pushed me forward. Or maybe I just wanted to see her.

She leaned against the wall beside the front door, her hair long and free—the way I liked it. Her shoulders were bare and so were her legs, and I took a good long look before meeting her eyes.

For a few seconds, there were no words. Hell, I barely breathed. That's the kind of power that sat in the depths of those clear eyes.

"Out for a drive?" I said slowly, as if I didn't give a shit.

Monroe took a step forward but paused, her hands swinging at her side. The dress was on the short side, and man, she looked hot in it. I tried to ignore the pull I felt toward her, but it was damn hard. Especially when she moved a piece of hair behind her shoulders and sighed.

"You could say that."

"You look like you're dressed for a party or something."

"Oh," she tripped over her words, "I…this was all I had and…"

I didn't want to do this. Not with her. I just wanted the truth.

"What's going on, Monroe?"

She took another step and I shoved my hands into my front pockets, shoulders hunched, a ferocious scowl in place.

"I'm sorry," she said softly.

"For what?" Something cracked loose inside me, something heavy. It broke away like a chunk of rock falling from a cliff, and suddenly I felt lighter than I had all week.

Was it the sound of her voice? Did she have that kind of power? Or was it the fact that being near her for less than five minutes had me wanting to crush her to my chest and just breathe in that summery, gentle smell.

The crap week I'd had melted away, and though I felt my resolve failing, I didn't want her to get off easy. I wanted her to squirm a bit.

"I'm sorry for the silent treatment this week. I…" She licked her lips and my focus shifted slightly. How could it not? She had on this light gloss that looked wet and soft. All I could think about was the kiss we'd shared and how amazing it had felt.

"When things get intense, I pull away." She shrugged. "It's what I do. It's how I cope."

Okay. I got that. I mean, it didn't make me feel better or anything, but at least I understood.

"So why are you here?"

A soft blush swept across her cheeks, and she twirled a strand of hair between her fingers. "Well, I guess I'm hoping that you might want to hang out…" Her voice trailed away as our eyes connected. "Or something," she whispered.

The grandfather clock at the end of the hall decided to chime eight bells, and she flinched at each one. When the echo died, I spoke quietly.

"Is this a date?" I asked, watching her closely. I loved how easy it was for me to make her blush.

She shook her head. "Not really. I mean, I don't know."

"So what is it then?"

"Does it have to be something? Can't it just be a couple of friends hanging out?"

"So we're friends now?"

The air thickened. Or maybe my lungs stopped working, because I had trouble breathing, and I thought that just maybe the look in her eyes wasn't a look you'd give a friend. It was way too hot for that.

It made me wonder what she saw reflected in my eyes, because I sure as heck felt hot and tight, and there was the whole trying to breathe normally thing.

"We're friends," she said softly. "Friends who don't date."

Her eyes slid from mine, and she twirled a piece of hair nervously.

"Give me five minutes and I can be ready for our second 'non-date.' I gotta grab a quick shower."

"Okay," she said hesitantly, and I knew she wasn't exactly sure what had just happened.

"And Monroe?"

"Yes?"

I couldn't help the slow grin that spread across my face. It was a side effect of the lightness inside me. A lightness that, these days, only she seemed to be able to tap into.

"I'm glad you stopped by."

# Chapter Seventeen

# Monroe

"Two Saturdays in a row," Nate said as he slid into Gram's car and reached for his seat belt. He'd had the quickest shower ever and reappeared in less than ten minutes, wearing a pair of faded jeans, beat-up brown boots, and a steel-blue, long-sleeved Henley.

He looked way too good, and my heart started beating a mile a minute as soon as I saw him.

I'm sure he heard it, which was why I turned without saying anything and bolted for the car. I managed a wave at his mom and dad, but I'm sure they thought I was a complete idiot.

"Monroe?"

"What?" I glanced at him, and anything else I was going to say kind of froze in my throat.

His hair was damp and hung to the top of his shoulders in tangled waves that told me he hadn't taken the time to comb them properly. He tilted his head to the side a little, a half smile on his face, and ba-boom, there went my heart again.

My hands clutched the steering wheel as if it was a lifeline, but I kept picturing them trailing across the stubble on his chin, and even though I'd told myself I wouldn't go there again, I thought of the kiss we'd shared. I swear I could close my eyes and feel his lips on mine.

"Are you okay?"

I glanced at him. Took a few moments. And then I was able to speak. "Yep." I nodded and put the car in reverse. "Perfect. Right as rain."

Oh God. I was rambling. This wasn't good.

I pulled out onto the road and headed toward town. The sun was just starting to descend, and the horizon was filled with red-gold rays. I had the windows down and smelled a hint of rain in the air. And though it was still hot and sticky, I was cold.

And nervous.

So. Freaking. Nervous.

"So where are we going?"

*Shit.*

"To town."

"To do what?"

"Hang out."

"Hang out where?"

I had a death grip on the wheel by now. "What's with all the questions?"

I felt his gaze on me but refused to look at him. I concentrated on the road and didn't even protest when he changed the radio station. I was driving, so technically the music choice was my call, but hey, he could knock himself out because I had other things on my mind.

What was I doing? I knew he was going to hate the Coffee House. I knew the idea was a bad one. I knew this and yet…

*I wanted to see him.*

Unease settled in my gut, and I felt my cheeks heat again. This must be some kind of record.

I'd wanted to see Nate, and this had been my excuse. It had been my way of getting around the fact that I'd been a total asshole, ignoring him after Sunday. After that kiss.

After that kiss that had made my head spin and my limbs feel like spaghetti. A kiss that had twisted me up in heat and fear and desire, making me feel all sorts of things. Making me *feel*. And the weird thing was? I'd liked it a lot.

And that made me wonder just what it was that I had gotten myself into.

We drove through town and I followed the directions in my head—the ones Brent had given me when he'd called earlier. I drove to the end of the main drag and turned left onto Fossil Street, biting my lip when Nate sat taller and glanced my way.

"Where are we going, Monroe?" His voice wasn't friendly anymore. In fact, it was downright harsh, and I bit my lower lip so hard I tasted blood as I took my foot off the accelerator and began to slow down.

I cleared my throat, an exaggerated sort of thing that had

me wincing, and pulled the car into a parking spot. What was I going to say to him? Shoot. *Think, Monroe.*

I yanked out the key and turned to him. Crap. He looked angry.

"Don't be mad."

Wow. That was a great start.

His eyes were flat, his mouth tight and tense. "I'm guessing we're not here because you want to go to Chuck E. Cheese."

"No."

Nate ran his hands through his hair and glanced out the window, across the street to the Coffee House. There was a patio out front and it was filled with people. Mostly teenagers, a few I recognized from the bush party.

"I ran into Brent today."

He said nothing, his eyes still on the Coffee House, and I shivered, my skin damp from the humidity. How was I going to fix this?

"We can go somewhere else if you want," I offered.

"Where did you see Brent?"

"Oh, at the, uh, market. He was buying stuff for his mom and I was there with Gram. He told me that it would be a good time and that he and the other guys you jam with would be here. I thought…"

"Clearly you weren't thinking."

No. Clearly I wasn't.

I exhaled and drummed my fingers along the steering wheel, not really sure what to do or say.

"I can take you home," I said slowly.

"I don't want to go home."

*Okay.*

"Well, where do you want me to take you?"

"I don't want you to take me anywhere."

Nate was pissed, and though I couldn't really blame him, the snark in his voice still stung.

"Well, that's pretty vague."

"It's all I got," he snapped.

"I'm sorry, I didn't mean to make you angry."

His eyes were flat. "I don't want this shit pushed on me."

"I'm sorry—"

"Quit saying you're sorry. You're not sorry. How can you be sorry when you just don't get it?"

Hurt, for a moment I couldn't get the words out, and when I did, my voice was tremulous and weak.

"You're not the only one who's been through shit, you know."

He yanked his hand through his hair, his eyes glittery and angry. "Look, you brought me here. I didn't ask to come, but Jesus, Monroe, did you really think this was gonna be a good idea? I know I'm not the only one dealing with crap. I heard you the other night. Your mistake died? Is that it? Does that make your shit worse than mine?"

Pain lashed across my chest so tightly that, for a moment, I couldn't breathe. I looked away, afraid that I was going to lose it big-time, and I tried to still the trembling in my fingers.

"I can't believe you just said that." My words were barely a whisper. How had everything fallen apart already?

I stared across the street for the longest time, not really knowing what to do or say. Nate was right. This was my fault. I *had* brought him here. I must have known this wasn't going to end well, so why had I done it? What was wrong with me?

Me, Monroe Blackwell, the person who didn't like to feel anything, and now I was so full of emotion I was choking on it. It hurt.

I'd forgotten how much it could hurt.

Brent poked his head out of the door and I watched him look across the street at us. He lifted his hand, gave a half wave, beckoned for us to come, and then disappeared back inside with most of the crowd following him.

It was after nine, so I knew they were getting ready to play.

I watched a couple walk along the sidewalk, the guy with his arm across the girl's shoulder, leaning into her, laughing, talking, kissing her neck as they headed toward the Coffee House.

They looked happy. Carefree.

Something else ripped through me in that moment, and it took a few seconds for me to get what it was. Jealousy.

I had to look away. I had to bury it or choke.

"I'm going in," I said quietly. "You can come with me, or wait in the car, or you can leave. I really don't care."

Except that I did. I cared a lot.

I yanked on the door, slammed it shut, and crossed the street without looking back. What was the point?

I was alone.

# Chapter Eighteen

# Nathan

I waited in Monroe's car for about twenty minutes. I sat there, pissed off at everything. Monroe. Brent. Myself. Trevor. The Coffee House.

I watched guys I knew walk in with their guitars, and it was hard not to get out and walk in the other direction. I couldn't fathom hearing and feeling the music without Trevor. I didn't think I could stand it.

And yet, there was a part of me that was tired of fighting all of it, and I suppose it was that part of me that propelled me forward. I got out of the car, but instead of heading in the opposite direction, I found myself crossing the street.

Out here, near the patio, I could hear Brent singing—or trying to sing. The guy was great for background vocals, but he didn't have the chops to carry anything on his own. He hit a particularly difficult note—a high C—and I winced.

"Please tell me you're going in?"

Janelle, one of the waitresses, wiped up the last table and nodded toward the door. With the music on, the patio was empty.

I didn't answer her because I wasn't sure.

"I hope you do, hon," she said before heading to the door. "I'm pretty sure Trevor would want you up on that stage."

I wasn't so sure of that. I thought that maybe, if Trevor was here right now, he'd want to knock me on my ass. And I'd let him.

She disappeared inside, and I stared after her until my eyes blurred. I took a step but froze because I couldn't go inside. Not yet.

I slid into a chair and leaned forward, resting my hands on my knees as I gazed at the stone floor. My shoulders felt heavy. So did my feet, like my boots were encased in cement or something. The air was damp, and I shivered as a wave of laughter rolled through the Coffee House.

Someone was speaking, Brent maybe, but the words were muffled—it sounded as if he was talking underwater.

For a second, with my eyes closed, I went back in time. Back to last summer when Trevor, Brent, and I would spend every other Friday night inside, playing until our fingers felt like they were gonna fall off.

Trevor could pick apart any song we wanted to play. And his voice, man, we sounded good together. When the two of us were in the moment, when that rush of adrenaline pumped through our veins, when the crowd chanted and clapped because they wanted more—it was heaven.

There was nothing like it.

I wondered if he heard anything now. If, when he was alone, unable to speak or to communicate…did he hear stuff? Did he think of all these things from before? Did he wonder why he was in a hospital bed, frozen in time? Broken. Damaged.

"Jesus," I muttered and ran a hand through my hair. It was still damp from the shower, and as I leaned back and gazed up at the starless sky, I heard Brent and his buddy break into an old Skynyrd song.

My fingers began to move, and as Brent found his place, his comfort zone, he began to belt out the lyrics. A little off key, but there was something there nonetheless, and I heard the crowd singing along.

I was up on my feet before I knew what I was doing, crossing the patio and pushing the door open.

A wall of heat hit me.

The Coffee House was full—standing room only—and even though the tables had candles burning, it was dark. Dark and intimate. Just like I remembered.

It was a great place to be. You could find a dark corner and get busy with your girl while enjoying the tunes.

I closed my eyes for a second, knowing that the coffee bar was to my left. That over the top of the door leading to the kitchen there was a fake talking parrot. I knew that if you asked it a question, it would answer with something nasty.

I knew that Mr. J would be back there cooking and that his wife, Macy, would be serving up coffees and lattes, their daughter Kristy helping out. I knew that if I went over to the coffee bar, Kristy would try to slip me her cell number and her mom would frown but pretend that she hadn't seen anything.

In here, the sounds were the same as before. The smells. Cinnamon. Chocolate. The muted voices, the music. The vibrations along the floor.

Nothing had changed and yet, as Brent sang a Foos song, his voice cracking a little, I felt the weight of my world crushing me from the inside out. I felt the weight of my existence.

The weight of *my* change.

Someone bumped into me and I moved forward, sliding through the crowd gathered along the edges. It was three bodies deep here, and I nodded at a few girls who waved, not stopping to talk. My eyes scanned for Monroe, and I found her near the stage.

She was sitting at a table, just in front of Brent. And she was alone.

Brent grinned when he saw me, and I felt a bit of that weight lift, though when Monroe followed his gaze, I kind of froze.

Her large, expressive eyes didn't waver as I took another step closer. Someone grabbed my arm and I glanced to the side, irritated. It was Rachel.

"Hey, Nate," she said. Her eyes were glassy and her smile was lopsided. She was high. "Come sit with me."

"It's not gonna happen, Rachel."

Her eyes narrowed a bit and she looked past me toward

Monroe. "So that's her? That's the girl you took to the festival?" Her voice trembled a bit and I felt bad. Some kids were looking our way, elbowing each other and waiting for something big to happen. Rachel had never had a filter when it came to public scenes. The girl liked it when everyone was watching.

"Rachel," I groaned, so not in the mood for a fight.

"She's pretty," Rachel said. "Real pretty."

Surprised, I gazed down into her eyes. She had a wild look about her that went beyond being high. "Are you all right?" It didn't matter that we weren't together anymore—she would always be my first girlfriend and I cared about her.

"No, but as soon as Brad Lawson gets me out of here, I'll be flying."

Brad Lawson. No surprise there. At one time, the thought of her with that douche bag would have driven me crazy, but now...now I just wanted her to be safe and to not hate me.

"I'm sorry, Rachel. I don't want to hurt you, I just…"

"So that's it?" she asked. "We're really over."

"It wasn't good for a long time," I replied softly.

"I know," she replied. "I know," she said again. "But it doesn't make me feel any better to see you here with her."

"It's not what you think."

"Oh?" she said. "What is it exactly?"

I glanced back toward Monroe and found her eyes on me. I shrugged. "I don't know." But it could be something big, I thought.

"Well," Rachel said. "Maybe you should figure it out."

We stared at each other for a long time, and then she reached up and hugged me, her mouth near my ear. "I miss you. Please tell me we can at least be friends." She pulled away and looked up at me. "No one knows me like you do, Nathan, and I...I don't want us to act like strangers, you know? It would just be wrong." She sighed. "It would be so wrong. After everything. After Trevor."

"I know."

And then her friend Gia grabbed her arm and dragged her away from me.

After a few seconds, I turned and slid through the crowd, not stopping until I was inches from Monroe.

"I'm sorry," I said, hating the way her eyes fell away from me.

For a second, I thought I'd blown everything. I thought my need to hurt and to lash out had ruined whatever it was that we had.

But then she moved her chair, and I knew things were going to be all right. A bit more of that weight left me, and I slid in beside her.

Brent and his buddy broke into some kind of hillbilly crap that Trevor would have loved, and after a few seconds, I relaxed enough to sit and watch. Link, the drummer in our band, was a table over and grinned, his arm around a redhead. I nodded but kept my focus on Brent.

Monroe and I didn't talk or even look at each other, but when my hand crept over hers, she didn't move away. Her fingers were cool and I loved how they fit inside mine. I felt as if I'd just won the war or something.

Brent played for nearly twenty minutes more, his eyes laughing as the girls up front sang along to everything that came out of his mouth. His buddy, a guy I vaguely knew from a town in the next parish, was pretty good, and by the time they were done, I was completely relaxed.

Was it the music? Maybe. Though I'm guessing it had more to do with the fact that Monroe's hand was still in mine and her bare thigh was pressed up against my leg.

Brent finished off with a flamboyant chord run and then leaned over to whisper something to his buddy. The guy slid from his chair and jumped off the stage, his eyes on me, his guitar outstretched.

"Hey guys, why don't y'all make a lot of noise and maybe we can convince Everets to get his ass up here and play for us." Brent was standing, clapping his hands and gesturing to the crowd behind me.

His buddy grinned. "Dude, you should get up there."

Monroe nudged me with her leg and I glanced down at her.

"I'd love to hear you play," she whispered.

My eyes moved from her shining eyes down to her mouth. To her lips that were slightly glossed and so damned kissable they should be illegal. I thought of the week before. I thought of our kiss.

And I thought of what she'd said.

I jumped up and grabbed the guitar that was held in front of me, but before taking the stage beside Brent, I bent forward, my mouth close to her ear.

"I'll play for you, Monroe. Just for you. But remember it will cost you."

She shivered a little, and I tucked a strand of hair behind her ears as I straightened. The weight that was on my shoulders was nearly gone, and the girl in front of me was the reason for it. I knew that it would come back. It would come back with a vengeance, but I was willing to forget about it for tonight.

I was willing to see where this was gonna take me.

"Huh," she said huskily. "What's the price?"

I chuckled, a grin in place as someone let loose a long wolf whistle.

"I play for you and in return, I want that kiss."

"Kiss?"

"Yeah. The one you promised. I'm gonna collect tonight."

# Chapter Nineteen

# Monroe

I could have watched Nathan play his guitar and sing all night.

He was that good. No. He was better than good. He was charismatic and hot and sexy and talented and…

I shivered just thinking of how he'd bent low over the mike, guitar cradled in his hands when he sang, and of how his eyes had never left me for the entire time he'd been onstage.

Not once.

He was riveting, and I was still buzzing from the high I'd gotten watching him perform. Still buzzing from what he'd said to me.

It was just after midnight by the time we pulled up to Nate's place. There was no moon and no stars, so it was pretty dark. I stopped the car behind his father's truck and tried to swallow the lump in my throat.

Have you ever tried to swallow something that was as big as a freaking golf ball? It's not fun. Especially when you're trying to act like everything is cool, when clearly, everything isn't.

It was the total opposite of cool. It was hot. And scary. And exciting. And did I say hot?

My hair stuck to the back of my neck and I pushed at it impatiently, exhaling as I tried to wipe my damp palms along my dress without him noticing.

Nate hadn't made a move to collect his *payment* yet, and I was pretty sure now was it.

I rotated my shoulders and glanced up at his house. It was as dark as everything else. His parents had either gone out themselves or they were in bed already. Either way, it felt like there was no one around for miles.

"Are you gonna shut this thing off?"

"What?" I jumped at the sound of his voice. The little bit of light from the dashboard illuminated his face—his strong chin, high cheekbones, and a mouth that made me think of things.

It made me think about the kiss we'd shared the week before. And what his body had felt like pressed up against mine. With his longish hair and that little bit of stubble on his chin, he looked dangerous. He looked *hot*.

And though he looked perfect, I knew that he was as un-perfect as I was. We were damaged, the two of us, in ways not a lot of people could understand. And for the first time since all the bad stuff had happened to me, I didn't feel so alone. I didn't feel like the freak with too much shit inside her. The one who couldn't talk. The one who fell into herself and hid.

I felt almost…normal.

I felt like a girl, sitting in a car with a boy. A boy who she liked.

I turned the key and settled back in my seat, not sure what to do or say, and for the first time, the monumental inexperience of my life hit me in the face.

*I bet Rachel would have no problem knowing what to do.*

I'd seen her grab Nate at the Coffee House. I didn't have to be introduced to know she was his ex-girlfriend. She'd looked at Nate as if he was a yummy piece of chocolate. One that she'd tasted. And when she looked my way, I could tell that she still wanted him.

She was exactly as I'd imagined. Tanned. Blond. And gorgeous. Every guy's fantasy, and yet, he was here with me.

"Thanks," Nate said suddenly.

"For what?"

"I was a total dick tonight. Thanks for not leaving."

The radio was on low, an old song by The Fray, and for a few seconds, we listened to it, Nate's fingers tapping along the tops of his knees while he hummed the melody.

"Trevor was such a pussy when it came to music, ya know?"

My head rested against the back of the seat and I turned slightly so that I could see him.

"What do you mean?"

"The Fray. Good band. Solid songwriting skills with a lot of melody, but not a whole lot of guitar and drums. I like heavy guitar and loud aggressive drums. Five Finger Death Punch is more my speed." Nate shook his head, his eyes ahead and his mind elsewhere. "But Trevor loved The Fray. He was real big on melody, and it's why we worked together so well. It's why we clicked. I was all about technique and arpeggio scales and fast riffs, but he kept things in perspective, he smoothed things out, and together, man, we wrote some good songs."

That surprised me and I sat up a little straighter.

"You wrote your own stuff?"

Earlier, at the Coffee House, Nate had played a bunch of songs with Brent, showing off some impressive guitar skills while singing all of the girls into a frenzy. He had something real special, and though it had taken a few songs for him to open up, once he did, I was mesmerized.

He'd made me feel as if I was the only girl in the room, and I'm pretty sure every other girl had felt the same way. How could they not? When he looked at me, I felt as if he was touching something inside me and that something was alive. It was hot and aching and a little scared.

I wanted to be touched. I wanted to feel. And maybe to forget.

"Yeah," he answered softly, bringing me back. "We wrote a lot. Some of it was crap, but some of it was pretty good. We were gonna record them this summer, maybe put them up on iTunes or something…"

Nate sighed and I felt his pain. I felt it cross my chest and hit me hard like an old friend saying hello.

"We were gonna go for it. Even talked about moving to LA or New York when we graduated. And now…"

He shuddered and ran his hands along the tops of his legs. Back and forth. And then again.

"Shit," he muttered. "How did I end up here?"

For a moment, I panicked. "Here with me?"

"No," he answered. "Just here...here looking down a road that I don't recognize anymore. A road that I never thought I'd be on, you know? Trevor was supposed to be with me. It was always us against everyone else. Us and our music."

"Nate, you can't give up on your dreams. You don't know what's going to happen. None of us do. Trevor could wake up tomorrow." But I knew the likelihood wasn't great. I'd heard Gram talking to one of her friends the day before. I'd heard words like sepsis, brain damage, possible infection.

"It doesn't matter what I say or think, Monroe. There is only the truth. And the simple truth is that Trevor is laid up in a hospital because of me. He might never wake up *because of me*. Or if he does, he might be screwed up so badly he might wish he'd just died. It sucks, and I can't change a thing, no matter how bad I want to."

He scrubbed at his eyes angrily, pushing his hair off his face. "It's not fair. It's not fair because I'm sitting in a car on a hot summer night with a beautiful girl. I'm smelling her shampoo and imagining what it would feel like to hold her. I'm feeling things I shouldn't be feeling, because I don't deserve them."

He swore again. "But what makes it worse is that I *want* to be here with you and that makes me feel like crap. It makes me feel guilty. I feel…"

He looked at me, and my heart melted a little more when I saw moisture in the corners of his eyes. I undid my seat belt and moved closer, my eyes not leaving his. My heart felt like it was gonna beat right out of my chest, it roared in my ears, heavy and strong and…

*Alive.*

I reached for him, my palm on his cheek, and my heart turned over when he leaned into me. He closed his eyes, and I gently wiped away the single tear that fell.

"What do you feel?" I asked so softly I barely heard myself, and at first, I thought that maybe the words had only echoed inside my head.

His hands moved into my hair, and I couldn't move if I wanted to. When my eyes focused, I gazed into his. I saw the pain that lay there. The anguish and the sorrow. But I saw something else.

"Do you have to ask?" he said hoarsely.

I stared into his eyes for so long that my vision blurred. His fingers wrapped around my skull, tangling in my hair and pulling me even closer. I smelled mint gum and something subtle, but nice.

It was hot in the car, but his body heat made it ten times more so, and my dress clung to my skin, my hair to the back of my neck.

He rested his forehead on mine and drew in a ragged breath

that I felt deep in my own lungs. Every single inch of me felt as if it was on fire. Hot. Achy. Tremulous.

I swear my limbs had melted into rubber the moment he touched me, and I was afraid that if he let go, I'd pitch forward.

My hands crept up his chest. I felt his beating heart and the heat from his body through his shirt, and he groaned a little when I continued upward until I wrapped them around his neck. I couldn't think about anything other than getting closer to him. I shifted my hips and he moved so that I was practically sitting in his lap.

"God, Monroe. This is so wrong."

No way was it wrong. It was so right.

I had to swallow that damn lump again, and when I did, I managed to croak. "Why?"

"It's so wrong to *feel*, to be with you when Trevor is—"

"Stop it," I said loudly, pushing at him once and then again until he was forced to look into my eyes. "What happened is done. You can't change anything, Nate. At some point, you're going to have to forgive yourself and just…live again."

Holy hell. If my therapist could hear me now, he'd be fist-pumping his way to the freaking moon.

"Is that what you're doing, Monroe? Have you forgiven yourself?"

For a few moments, there was no sound other than the breeze buffeting the hood of the car and our breaths falling in short, hard spurts. Images I didn't ever want to see flashed before my eyes, and I shook my head violently.

"I don't want to talk about Malcolm."

For a second, he said nothing and then he exhaled and I could feel him pulling away, but I needed something more. *He* needed something more.

"I haven't forgiven myself. I don't think I ever will but…" I paused as the enormity of the words in my head washed over me. They pressed into my chest and made it hard to breathe or speak.

When I spoke again, it was barely a whisper. "I'm learning to live again, and that's a start."

"It's hard," he said, his dark eyes hooded, his gaze on my mouth.

My hands encircled his neck, and I felt his fist in my hair as I bent forward. "I know," I breathed into him, my mouth hovering above his.

Our noses touched, and my breath caught at the back of my throat. I think I whimpered or maybe I sobbed. I don't know. I couldn't hear. I could barely function.

Because when he moved enough so that his lips were on mine, everything stopped except us.

There was nothing but Nathan and this hot Louisiana night. There was nothing but the need to connect to someone so badly I felt it ache in every part of my body.

His mouth was warm, his lips firm as he slid them over mine. Bombs could have been going off for all I knew, because it sure as heck felt like it. My world was rocking and I was letting it.

Nate's scent, the feel of his hair between my fingers, his hard chest and legs beneath my body—all of it rushed through me.

And oh God, could he kiss.

I opened my mouth beneath his and he groaned into me, shifting yet again so that now I straddled him. I let him kiss me with all the ferocious need and anguish inside him, and I have no idea how long we were like that—connected on every level, touching each other, tasting each other—and when he broke away, I whimpered again.

"Don't stop," I said throatily, running my hand across his jaw.

"Monroe, if I don't stop," he said huskily. "If we don't…" Something like pain crossed his face, and suddenly I was aware of a few things.

My skirt had ridden up to my hips, and the bright pink boy undies I had on were there for him to see. In fact, one of his hands was on the small of my back, holding me in place.

Holding me against him.

*Against him.*

"Shit," I said, wriggling like mad to move away. By the look on his face, I think I made things worse. "I'm sorry."

I kneeled on the seat beside him, biting my lip and not sure what to do. His arm slipped around me, pulling me into his warmth.

"I just need a minute."

"Okay."

*So do I.*

Holy hell, so did I.

It might have taken more than a few minutes for our hearts to settle, and by then I realized that it was nearly 1 a.m. and Gram was expecting me.

"I have to go."

"I know." He kissed the top of my head and I smiled. "One more minute."

"Just one?" I teased.

"I'd take more, but I don't want to get on Mrs. Blackwell's bad side."

I giggled and snuggled into him. "She likes you. I don't think you have to worry."

"Good to know." I smiled at the lightness in his tone. "And Monroe?"

I angled my head so I could see him. "Yes."

"Technically that wasn't my collection kiss."

My smile widened. "It wasn't."

He shook his head. "Nope. Rules are you have to state the claim before the prize is collected, and I didn't state my claim."

I liked this side of him. The light side. The teasing side. And I liked how he made me feel. Coyly, I grinned. "So I guess I owe you at least one more kiss."

There was a pause.

My heart sped up.

"At least."

# Chapter Twenty

# Nathan

"So, as per the rules, I'm stating my claim."

It was Sunday night and getting kind of late, but I couldn't help myself. I had to hear her voice, and I needed to see her even more.

I'd spent most of the day and night at a family thing at my aunt and uncle's. Yep. The entire day spent with a bunch of cousins who were either too young and annoying to hang with or too old and annoying to hang with.

So I'd pretty much kept to myself. My family thought I was brooding—angsting over my situation—and I was fine with that. Because as long as they did, they didn't try to talk to me and I could be alone with my thoughts.

Thoughts that went from X-rated to kind of pissed off to confused—and all of them were about Monroe.

I'd thought about how amazing it had felt to hold her and how much I wanted to do more than just kiss her. I thought of her laugh and the way it lightened everything, especially the heaviness inside me.

And I thought about Malcolm.

Who was he? A friend? A boyfriend?

I wanted her to share her secret with me. To trust me enough to do it. But I was willing to bet that Monroe would only come around when she was ready. And maybe she would never be ready.

"So when exactly are you collecting your prize?"

Monroe's voice cut through my thoughts and I grinned.

"Tonight."

"Tonight? But it's nearly midnight and I'm already in bed."

"Really," I said, my grin widening. "And what does Monroe Blackwell wear to bed?"

She giggled, a soft, girlish sound that made my gut churn with anticipation.

"Guess you'll never know."

I grabbed my knapsack from my bed and shook my head. "Don't count on it. See you in a bit."

"What do you mean by that?"

"Guess you'll have to wait and see," I answered before pocketing my cell and heading out of my room.

The house was dark—my parents had gone to bed as soon as we'd come home—and I crept through it silently. They'd never been super strict with me. I don't think they'd ever given me a curfew, but considering everything that had happened this year, I was pretty sure they wouldn't be too happy catching me sneaking out of the house at midnight.

I still couldn't drive—my license was suspended until the fall—but that didn't mean my dad's bike was off limits. Slipping the backpack over my shoulders, I climbed aboard and set off for Oak Run Plantation.

The sky was clear, and my eyes adjusted quickly, so traveling the back roads was easy.

Would she like what I had planned? Or would she think it was stupid? Corny.

I thought of the connection we had shared the night before, and I had to believe that she would get it. I had to believe that Monroe would understand, 'cuz if not, I was gonna look like a total effing loser. The fact that I was *willing* to look like a total effing loser meant something, but right now I wasn't going to think about it too much.

I rode up the silent driveway, noting the low light that fell from the main plantation house, though Mrs. Blackwell's cottage was in darkness. The night felt electric. I heard the cicadas buzzing, the sad hoot of an owl close by, and the always humid, damp air filled with the scent of honeysuckle and whatever else Mrs. Blackwell had growing in her gardens.

I jumped off the bike and set it against the porch. Took one step up and froze.

Already erratic, my heart began to thump like a kick drum— fast and heavy. Ba-boom, ba-boom, ba-boom.

God, what was it about this girl that had me all twisted up?

I couldn't see her face—it was in shadow—but her hair spilled over her white T-shirt like long fingers of ink. She leaned against the edge of the railing, wearing cut-off jean shorts and runners.

"Hey," she said slowly, a husky tone in her voice that I liked.

I took two more steps up until my head was level to hers. This close, I could see her features, the reflection of the stars in her eyes, the moisture along her bottom lip as if she'd just licked it.

I leaned forward and brushed my mouth against hers. Couldn't help myself. But it was a quick one. We had to hurry.

"You ready?" I asked, my hand seeking hers and tugging her down the steps with me.

"For what?" She sounded breathless.

I didn't answer. We trudged along the side of the house and I made my way over to the maze. It was freshly trimmed—I know because I'd done it the week before—and I knew my way around it.

I didn't stop until we were in the center, and pausing, I glanced up at the sky, nodding to myself as I let go of Monroe's hand and reached for my backpack.

"Nate, what are we—"

"Hold on," I said, grabbing her once more and planting a kiss on those lips. It only lasted a few seconds and it took everything I had to break it off.

I whipped out a worn blanket, one I'd taken from my bed, and spread it over the grass. Then I motioned for Monroe to lie down.

She arched one of those delicate eyebrows, a soft smile on her face, but pulled off her shoes and then knelt on the blanket, moving over when I did the same.

"So, a midnight picnic?" she said, nudging me with her elbow.

I shook my head.

"No?" she grinned. "I don't think Gram will like us camping out together overnight."

"I only need you for a few hours."

"A few hours," she repeated.

Damn, but I liked to see her smile. It made me feel like a king.

I lay down, and for a moment, she stared down at me, her expression unreadable, and I could tell she was a little nervous.

"I'm not going to bite you."

"I know," she answered quickly. "You're going to kiss me."

"Yep. That I am." I reached up and grabbed her arm, tugging her down until she was sprawled across my chest. Her hair hung loose, obscuring her face and tickling my nose. Her scent was all around me. It was in me, and I felt it as if it was alive. As if it made me alive.

She was so warm, so soft, and with a groan, I rolled her over so that she was beside me, on her back and tucked into my arms.

For a few seconds, her breaths fell rapidly, little puffs of mist that hung in the air and then disappeared like the fireflies along the edge of the maze.

"What are we doing out here, Nate?"

"Just wait. You'll see."

"See what?"

I pointed to the sky and turned to watch her as she followed my finger. I'd already seen the beginning of the meteor shower as I'd pedaled like a crazy person to get here, but according to the reports online, the big show was just about to start.

We lay like that for about ten minutes. Her body next to mine. Her breaths lifting me up. The soft sounds that fell from her lips were mesmerizing. This girl had her own rhythm, her own state of being, and it was addictive.

I could spend the entire night watching her.

I knew when the first wave of meteors broke through to our side because Monroe's eyes widened along with her smile. Only then did I look away and turn to the sky.

"Holy shit," she exclaimed. "What is this?"

"A meteor shower," I answered, watching the shooting sprays arc across the sky. The last time I'd watched one had been a few years back. Trevor and I and a few guys from the football team had gone out to Baker's Landing with a couple of six-packs. We'd stayed the night. Got wasted and watched the sky.

It had been pretty cool, but nothing compared to tonight. To being out here under an endless sky with Monroe tucked into my side like she belonged there.

We watched the light show for hours, it seemed, and when the dew fell and Monroe began to shiver, I pulled the blanket over us and wrapped us up like a cocoon. I felt…peaceful, and I would have stayed that way forever if I could have.

"It's beautiful," she murmured. "I'm not much of science nut, so I have no clue why they happen or what it is I'm seeing."

"It's the tail end of a comet coming close to our sun. The bits that fly off hit our atmosphere and," I nodded to the sky, "that's the result."

"Amazing," she whispered.

"Yeah."

I stared up into the sky and felt small. I felt small beneath its bigness and I wondered…

"Do you believe there's something out there?" I asked.

"What do you mean?"

*Stupid.* What the hell? Why was I getting all deep and shit?

"Nothing. Forget it."

She wriggled and loosened the blanket enough so that she could look at me. "Do you mean God?"

I shrugged but didn't answer, mostly because I didn't know what to say. The lightness was suddenly gone, and I was pissed that it was my fault.

"I believe there's something," she nodded, her pale eyes shimmery, like they were filling with tears.

Which made me feel worse.

She exhaled a long, shuddery breath and tried to smile, but it didn't really work. She looked so sad, so…broken.

"I used to think there was nothing. No one out there. No God." Her eyes squeezed shut. "Just nothing. But then I realized when you don't believe in anything anymore, what's the point of living? What's the point of breathing or water fights and summer picnics? What's the point of...loving?"

I didn't know what to say to that, so I was silent. I stroked her hair, and she relaxed against me again.

"There has to be something out there, some greater power, don't you think?"

"I guess so," I answered. My family wasn't overly religious, and I couldn't remember the last time I'd been to church. This kind of shit wasn't something I thought too much about, so why the hell had I brought it up?

"There *has* to be," she whispered. "I *need* for there to be. I need to believe that Malcolm is somewhere. That when he died, he didn't just end."

I wanted to know who Malcolm was. What happened? How did he die? And why did Monroe blame herself? I had so many questions, but I didn't ask any of them because I didn't feel as if I had the right to. I just stroked her hair and pulled her as close as I could.

"I'm sorry," I said. They were only two words, but they were all I had.

There was a pause.

"I know."

A heartbeat passed before she whispered, "I'm sorry too."

And then she began to cry.

# Chapter Twenty-One

# Monroe

I don't know how long I cried. I only know that when I finally stopped, I felt empty and my heart hurt.

Nate's arms, his warmth and strength, never left me, and for that I was grateful. I hadn't let this much emotion out since that awful day. In fact, I don't think I'd cried since. Not even at Malcolm's funeral.

My therapist had been trying to get me to this place—a place where denial didn't live and some sort of acceptance did.

A place where maybe I didn't blame myself. I'm not sure if I would ever really not blame myself for what happened that day, but I was one foot in that direction, which was one foot farther than I'd been.

Who knew that all it would take was a southern boy and a meteor shower?

I relaxed a bit. My face felt tight, and I was glad it was dark because I was pretty sure I looked awful. My eyes felt swollen, my tongue thick, and I knew how blotchy my pale skin got when I was upset.

I felt Nate's warm breath along the top of my head and turned slightly, resting on his chest with my eyes closed. I never wanted to leave here. If I could stay in his arms forever, I would, because right now, his forever was safe.

Several long moments passed. My chest tightened and then released as a wave of memories and images from that day crashed into me. I had only talked about it once, and even then, all of the little things—the things that mattered—I'd kept to myself.

But I didn't want to do that anymore.

"Malcolm was full of summer, you know? He looked like my dad, with wavy, blond hair and these big blue eyes that pretty much guaranteed he got away with a lot. He had dimples, freckles across his nose, and he bit the inside of his cheek sometimes. It used to drive my mom batty."

That was an understatement. My mom had tried everything to get him to stop, but nothing worked.

"It was hot that day."

Nate stiffened, inhaling deeply and then exhaling as he continued to stroke my head and hold me.

My eyes were squeezed shut, and though I was here with Nathan, in Louisiana, in my mind I was back in New York City. I saw the blinding, relentless sun and felt the heat on my cheeks as I hurried down the sidewalk so fast Malcolm could barely keep up. He'd worn a Batman T-shirt and faded cargo shorts.

I smelled the exhaust from the buses and taxis and cars.

Sausage from the vendors. Garbage piled up in the streets, waiting for the trucks to drive by and collect.

That afternoon, I'd been full of resentment and annoyance, and it killed me to remember those particular things. But I had to. I needed to get it out. I needed for Nate to understand even if I didn't.

Because Nate's pain was as real as mine, and maybe he could be saved. Maybe he'd never get to the place where I had been.

"It was wicked hot in the city, like record heat, and he wanted to go to the park. He'd bugged me about it all morning until I snapped. I thought he was doing it just because he knew I wanted to stay home. God, there was a *Walking Dead* marathon on, and I hadn't seen the show yet. I just wanted to chill and watch it with my best friend, who was in the Hamptons with her family."

I thought of my friend Kate. We would spend hours texting each other when we weren't together. Boys. Songs. Gossip.

But that day it was gonna be about zombies, and I hadn't seen her since the week before, so I was looking forward to painting my toenails, watching the zombies, and sharing all of it with her.

"Malcolm knew I didn't want to go, but he didn't care. I guess most seven-year-olds are kind of selfish that way."

I could have said no. I could have told Malcolm that the smog and humidity wasn't good for his asthma. But I didn't. At the time I thought, "Okay, you little twerp. We'll see how much you like it when you have trouble breathing."

It was mid-July, and there were weeks ahead of us. With Mom and Dad working until vacation in August, weeks where I was in charge. I wanted to teach him a lesson. I just didn't know it would all go so wrong.

"I remember Mick, the guy who sold sausages on the corner near the park, telling us we were crazy to be out." I paused. "He was right."

I had marched by, glaring at the back of Malcolm's golden head, and I had thought, "You little shit. Just wait, buddy. You should have listened to me."

"The funny thing was, when we got to the park, there were a lot of kids out. It was like a switch had been turned on or something. Malcolm gave me the biggest hug. His arms were thin—God, they looked like spaghetti noodles—but he was strong. He whispered in my ear, 'I love you, Roe,' and just like that, he made me feel like a total bitch for not wanting to bring him. I roughed up his hair a bit and told him he had an hour, tops."

I paused, overwhelmed, and then whispered. "He was fine with an hour. After all that, an hour at the park was enough for him."

Malcolm had run to the swings while I found a grassy spot under a tree and sat down. It was maybe a few degrees cooler but still so hot. I'd brought a book and lay down on my stomach to read. I didn't mean to fall asleep; it just kind of happened. I read a few pages. Texted with Kate and then closed my eyes.

"I would give anything," my voice broke, "*anything* to have not fallen asleep. I remember waking up and not knowing where

I was at first. I felt the breeze, smelled the grass, and heard the kids shrieking and giggling as they ran through the water pad on the other side of the swings. I don't know when I realized that something was wrong."

I shrugged and burrowed deeper into Nate's arms.

"Maybe it's why I woke up in the first place. Some weird sense that something was wrong."

I paused again, remembering how my stomach fell all the way to the ground and took me with it.

"I looked everywhere for Malcolm…but he was gone. I was frantic, yelling his name and shouting at the kids like a lunatic. This mother came over to me and asked me what was wrong. When I told her that my brother was missing, she looked around and then she shook my shoulders. She asked me when I'd seen him last and I told her…I told her that I'd fallen asleep and then I couldn't speak anymore. The look in her eyes…I'll never forget. She knew I had let it happen."

I thought that I was all cried out, but hot tears burned my itchy, blotchy skin.

"I screamed in her face. I yelled, 'It's not my fault,' but it was. And then when I found his inhaler in my bag, I just knew that something bad had happened. It was too hot. He needed his inhaler. By this time, the place was crawling with cops. I don't know who called them. It wasn't me. But they were there and they were asking me questions, and every time they did, I saw that woman's face. I saw her accusation."

My voice broke.

"I saw the truth."

"Oh God, Monroe. You don't have to do this," Nate breathed into me, his nose near mine, his dark eyes shiny.

But I did.

"They found him almost immediately, in the trees that cut through the park. I think he was trying to get back to me because he was in trouble, but I was asleep and totally unaware. I bet I yelled for me. He had to have, and sometimes I hear him, you know? I hear him screaming, 'Roe, where are you? Come get me!'

"He was already gone when they found him, and by then my mother had made it to the park." I shook violently at the memory. At the sound of my mother wailing. At the image of her pounding her fists into the police officer's chest. Her nails were scarlet. Blood red and pointy.

Funny the details you remember.

"The coroner told my parents later that he died because of a severe asthma attack, and I remember my mom asking about his inhaler. 'Where was his inhaler?' she kept asking, saying it over and over. I could never answer, but I think that she knows. I've never told her or my dad that I had his inhaler. That I still have his inhaler. I never told them that…"

I clung to Nathan, trying to block out the sounds of Malcolm's cries and the images of his face. My chest was so tight I could barely breathe, but eventually it fell away and I was nothing but a limp bag of bones and flesh.

"Jesus, Monroe. I'm so, so sorry."

I was hollow. Spent.

"Yeah," I answered slowly. "Me too."

## Chapter Twenty-Two
# Nathan

I woke up because the sun was in my eyes. It wavered for a bit and then disappeared again.

Shit. It was morning, and we were still in the maze. My hair was damp from the dew, but with Monroe still in my arms, burrowed beneath the blanket I'd brought, I was warm and dry.

It felt right somehow to be here with her, and I realized that for the first time in a long time, I was exactly where I wanted to be.

I don't think I slept much, but then how could I? I was still so angry for Monroe. I wanted to punch something. I wanted to smash and destroy and get rid of the anger inside me. It had festered and pulled real hard, just like it had the night after my accident when I'd woken up in the hospital, and Trevor didn't.

But I did none of that. I held Monroe until she'd fallen asleep, and then with no one but the lonesome owl nearby to hear me, I cried like a baby.

I cried for a little boy I'd never met and his sister who had come to mean everything to me in the space of a few weeks. I cried for Trevor. For his mom and dad. I cried like I hadn't cried since I was a kid in fourth grade and my collie, Abram, died. The bus had pulled up to my driveway, and there he was, lying in the middle of the road, killed by a car or truck.

I had to pull Abram out of the way for the bus driver, and I remember dragging his big body all the way to the porch, where I sat and cried until my dad came home.

We never got another dog after that, because me and my parents couldn't deal with the dying thing. Still couldn't. Here I was, nearly eighteen and still having trouble.

Everything fell out of me, and no one witnessed it except whoever the hell was up there, looking down on us. I wasn't sure if I liked him or not. I mean, what kind of God lets shit like this happen to little boys?

What kind of God lets someone like me get behind the wheel and destroy his best friend?

"Shit," I muttered, wincing as a ray of light fell into the center of the maze again, hitting me in the face like a big F U.

I guess it was his way of telling me that *He* didn't let any of us do anything. If we screwed up, it was on us. We had to own it. We could think. We could do.

It was up to us to make the right choices, but maybe it was up to Him to help with the fallout.

Maybe it was He who had sent Monroe to me.

Or maybe it was just fate.

Or maybe none of it was real. Maybe none of it mattered. Maybe I was so tired I couldn't think straight.

I tried to wiggle my legs a bit because my muscles were tight and cramped, but all I did was manage to send shooting pains up my thighs and to wake up Monroe.

She moved against me, her hair a wild mess that spilled over my chest. It took a few seconds to clear it from her face, and when she did, her eyes, those pale, crystal clear eyes, gazed up at me in a way that made my heart twist.

"Hey," she said, her voice raspy.

I didn't answer because nothing seemed to be big enough. No one word or phrase could cover what I was feeling. Instead, I bent forward and kissed her forehead, my hand seeking her jaw, and then I brushed the softness of her mouth.

"Thank you," she said softly.

I nodded and just held her for as long as I could. She didn't say anything else, and I was cool with that. Somehow, it was easier to confess and reveal when you were in the dark, but here in the early dawn, it was harder.

For now, holding her was enough. At least, I hoped it was enough for Monroe, because I would do anything to take away the pain I'd seen the night before.

Anything.

"Oh my God!" She squirmed and sat up. "We've been out here all night!"

Monroe rolled over and was on her knees before I had a chance to do or say anything.

"Gram is…I don't know what Gram is gonna say, but I need to get to the house now. Maybe she won't know I left. Maybe she's still in bed."

I nodded.

"Okay. Let's go."

It was Monday and I was due to be here in an hour or so anyway. I figured it was around six in the morning. I would have enough time to go home, eat breakfast, shower, and then start my day. But before I could do that, I had to make sure things were going to be cool between Monroe and her grandmother.

The meteor shower had been my idea, and though I hadn't meant for us to fall asleep, I liked waking up with Monroe in my arms. Any blowback would be worth it.

I packed up my bag. Tossed in the uneaten chips and Cokes I'd brought and then rolled up my blanket. When I glanced up, Monroe was staring down at me. I couldn't quite read her expression, and my gut twisted.

"What? Are you okay?" I asked, trying not to show panic, but man, she ripped me apart without even trying.

She nodded, a small, tremulous smile on her face. "I think so," she said almost carefully, as if she wasn't sure she should say anything at all. "I mean, I feel…lighter." She moistened her lips.

Slowly, I got to my feet. "Last night…" Shit, I needed to get this right. "I just want to make you better, Monroe. I don't want you to hurt anymore."

She stepped forward, slipped her arms around my waist, and rested her head on my chest. As soon as she touched me, my heart sped up and I buried my nose in her hair, loving the way she smelled. The way she felt.

"I haven't talked to anyone about Malcolm. Not even my therapist." Her breath hitched and my arms tightened.

"After it happened, I just wanted to forget everything about him. I wanted to forget how the sun made his hair look like liquid gold, or how, when he smiled, his dimples appeared like tiny little craters that I wanted to kiss. I wanted to forget how he'd made me so angry, and I wanted to forget how sorry I was. How guilty I was."

"It's okay."

She shook her head. "You don't understand, Nate. I couldn't even tell my parents the things they wanted to hear. The little details that told them he would be fine. After he died, they kept waiting for me to start talking...to start moving. I can see now how they existed in a state of nothing. They weren't moving forward. They weren't going back. They were just stuck in this horrible place, and they needed me to lead them out, but I couldn't. I wasn't strong enough. Instead I cut my wrist, which wasn't so much an attempt to kill myself as it was a way to make myself feel."

"Shit, Monroe." I lifted her chin. "I'm glad that you didn't..."

She sniffled. "It proved that I didn't feel anything. My parents sent me to therapy and they tried to get out of that place they were in. My dad started acting like everything was normal when it was so screwed up, and that made me angry. My mother...she just didn't know what to say or how to act, so she started avoiding me."

She squeezed her eyes shut.

"I get now that they were waiting for me. Waiting for me to come back to them. That they needed me before they could start to heal." Her eyes were shiny again, and she reached for me. She kissed me then, her mouth soft and tentative. I tasted the salt from her tears and the pain from her heart.

It was a slow, lingering kind of kiss that I wanted to keep going, because I could kiss this girl all day, but she pulled away and slipped her hand into mine. "We'd better go."

The birds sang as we trudged through the damp grass. We'd just rounded the corner of her grandmother's house and I was picking a twig out of Monroe's hair when the front door banged open and we both froze.

"A little early in the morning for a stroll, isn't it?"

Mrs. Blackwell leaned against the railing in a blue and white housecoat that fell almost to her feet. Matching slippers tapped along the floorboards, and she stared down at us with an expression that wasn't exactly pissed off, but it was something. What that something was I couldn't say at the moment.

She arched an eyebrow and pinched her lips when neither one of us answered right away.

Yeah. Okay, maybe she was pissed off.

"Mrs. Blackwell, I can explain. There was a meteor shower last night and I wanted Monroe to see it."

Her eyebrow arched a little higher.

"I called late and she, uh, I guess you were in bed and…"

Damn, that eyebrow was even higher now.

"Well, we kinda fell asleep in the maze," I finished, a smile pasted to my face. Usually a smile was enough to get any sort of female to melt a little bit. But she wasn't budging.

Though her eyebrow relaxed a bit, which made me feel a whole lot better.

"It's not Monroe's fault, so I hope if you're upset with anyone, it's me."

"I see," she said, eyeing my backpack and the state of our rumpled clothes. "Well, come on in then. I'll make you breakfast."

Breakfast.

"It's okay, ma'am. I'll just be heading home—"

"No, Nathan Everets, you will not. If I'm going to be upset with you, I'd rather do it over a pot of coffee and some bacon and eggs."

She gave us each a good long look and then slowly turned around, disappearing inside the house.

"Come on." Monroe tugged on my hand. "I wouldn't argue with Gram. She's pretty fierce and even though she looks sweet and maybe more frail than, say, a," she paused dramatically, "dragon, she's not."

"Is she pissed?"

"She's gotta be. At least a little."

"Should I be worried?"

"Probably." She tried to hide a grin. "Definitely."

Okay. Good to know.

# Chapter Twenty-Three
## Monroe

There are things in this world that will never surprise you. Things that are absolute. The sun rises each morning and sets in the evening. No surprise there.

The four seasons fall, one after the other. Again, no surprise.

I've learned in my sixteen and a half years that there are things that will surprise you because you don't see them coming. They can be hard, painful things, and it's those ones that will live with you forever, bound to your soul in layers that grow thicker each year. Hopefully those layers will eventually dull the pain.

There can also be awesome surprises. Again, ones you don't see coming, but when they find you, you wonder how you ever lived without them.

And sometimes, someone surprises you in a way that kinda knocks you on your ass. Nathan was one, but this afternoon it was Gram who held that honor.

After an amazing breakfast, spent watching Nathan do everything in his power to charm Gram, he left to go home for a quick shower and I'd been told that I was spending the day with Gram in *New Orleans*.

She said we were going to have a girls' day. That she wanted to shop for some new furniture, stuff for her porch and the newly refurbished one at the main plantation house.

Surprise number one. I was excited to go.

Surprise number two came just after we'd finished lunch at a cute little bistro and settled back into her old Matlock. She fired up the engine and turned down the radio.

"So, Monroe. Tell me something."

I buckled my seat belt, smoothed the hem of my yellow sundress, and glanced up.

"Yes?"

"Are you on the pill?"

Wait. What?

"The pill," I repeated. "Like the..." Jesus, I couldn't even say it. What was I? Twelve?

"Yes." She nodded. "The birth control pill."

*Shit.* Was I really gonna have the birds and the bees talk with Gram? First off, we covered that stuff in fifth grade and secondly, *seriously?*

I opened my mouth to say something, but since this was one of those surprises that rips into all of your normal thought processes, I didn't have anything. There were no words. There was just...

Hot cheeks, a sweaty brow, and suddenly a very dry mouth.

Gram pulled out into the road, signaling her turn, and stepped on the gas in precise, measured movements. She acted as if everything was normal and nice and as if she hadn't just asked me about…

"I'm just wondering is all. You did spend the entire night alone with a boy."

Now that I thought back, surprise number one had occurred at breakfast when she hadn't said one word about the fact that Nathan and I had spent the night in the maze. She'd let him ramble on and on about meteor showers and comets, and I spent the entire time watching him…just watching him.

Because he made me feel light.

So I suppose I shouldn't be surprised that she'd decided to corner me for the big "talk."

"Gram, that's…I'm not…I mean, we didn't."

"I'm not saying you did, honey, but as a young woman, you should be protected and so should he. And birth control pills aren't the only thing a young woman should have." She glanced at me and arched her eyebrow. "Condoms. You should have condoms as well."

*Oh. My. God.*

"Monroe, are you okay? You look pale."

"I'm good. I'm okay." I was so not okay.

I took a moment and then, well, I had to take another one. Gram had always been open with me, but still, hearing the word "condom" come out of her mouth was just *wrong*.

"So, if we did…I mean if I wanted to, you know, do that with Nathan, you wouldn't have a freak-out?"

"Monroe, stop putting words in my mouth. I would very much have a—" she navigated a turn and then glanced at me, "freak-out. But I also know that hormones, emotion, and a hot Louisiana night are a recipe for all kinds of things." She shook her head. "I may have gray hair and more than a few wrinkles on my face, but I remember what it feels like to be young and in love."

Jesus!

"I'm not in love with Nathan Everets," I said hotly. I mean, I couldn't be, could I? Didn't you have to know someone a lot longer than a few weeks to fall in love?

Oh God. Was that what all the heat and emotion and burning inside me was about? Was I in love?

"How do you know when you're in love?" I asked before I could stop myself.

Gram's eyes were straight ahead, the radio on low. "If you can't picture your tomorrow without a person in it? Then you're in love."

"Oh," I said shakily.

I glanced out the window, at the storefronts that blurred as we drove by, and tried to calm my suddenly frantic heart. It took a few moments, but eventually I settled against the seat.

"I told Nate about Malcolm."

Gram's eyes were on the road. She didn't say a word, but her right hand crept over to me and clasped mine in a tight grip. She didn't let go until we got to some old, rickety store that supposedly sold the finest antiques in the state of Louisiana.

With one hand, she maneuvered her big car into the smallest spot imaginable, something any trucker would be proud of. She cut the engine and squeezed my hand once more before letting go.

When she turned to me, her eyes were soft and pretty…but sad.

"I'm glad," she said haltingly.

"Me too."

I swallowed hard. "I miss him so much, Gram."

"I know."

The one question that had haunted me since that awful day pressed in hard. I tried not to think about it. I tried to concentrate on the sound that the fan made as it blew out cold air into the car. The radio was still on, the volume low, an old Elvis Presley song played. "Heartbreak Hotel."

Kind of appropriate.

"I want him to forgive me," I whispered. "Do you think he can?"

Her hand was on my cheek but my eyes were squeezed shut.

"Your brother loved you, Monroe. There was never anything to forgive. Remember that."

She stroked my hair and I let out a long, shuddering breath. It felt so good, her touch, her smell.

"Do you believe that everything happens for a reason?" I asked suddenly. I'd been given that line of bull from a lot of different people, and every time I heard it, I wanted to scratch their eyes out. I used to think they said something like that because they just didn't know what else to say.

I got that. What do you tell a teenager whose brother died on her watch? There were no words, no right thing to say.

"I believe in fate," Gram said softly. "And I believe in choice. Sometimes the two connect and sometimes they don't." She shook her head fiercely. "But Malcolm's death wasn't your choice, Monroe. Do you remember what I told you back then?"

Slowly, I nodded. I hadn't thought about that in forever.

"You told me that I would be fine. That Mom and Dad were going to be fine. That we would all get through this."

"Yes," she whispered. "And what else did I tell you?"

I had to think hard for a minute. There was so much about that day that I had pushed away. Stuff I didn't want to think about or remember ever again. Gram had been there with me for the worst of it, and I remembered her warmth, the scent of vanilla. And I remembered her tears.

"You told me that I was going to fall a long way down before someone caught me."

"Yes." Gram nodded slowly. "I begged your mother and father to let you come to me this summer because I truly believed it was time for you to come back to us. It was time, and I thought that I was going to be the one to catch you."

She shook her head and smiled. "But it wasn't me, my darling girl. It was Nathan. He caught you." She squeezed my hand again. "And I think that he's still waiting."

"For what?" I asked.

"Why, for you," she said in a very serious voice, before she opened her car door and glanced back at me. "To catch him."

# Chapter Twenty-Four

# Nathan

The week passed by in a blur of hot summer days spent out at the plantation working on a new gazebo with my uncle and hot summer nights spent under the stars with Monroe.

Working with my uncle was good for me. It was hard physical labor, and I wasn't the kind of guy who liked to sit on his ass and do nothing. Besides, there wasn't much time to think about shit when you were on a hot roof nailing tarpaper down.

There was no time to remember that night, to think about the stuff I should have done differently. The mistakes I'd made, the choices that had brought me to where I was.

Of course, Trevor was with me, but that was okay. I needed him there even if it was only in my head.

But it was those hot summer nights that I looked forward to, because it was those hot summer nights that made me forget everything but a girl with dark, silky hair and a mouth that I could spend hours kissing. Seriously, the girl could kiss, and over the last week, we'd had a lot of practice. *A lot.*

Sure, there might have been a bit of touching—okay, I knew that most of her was as soft and sweet as her mouth—but nothing else. And I was cool with that.

Monroe was different from any girl I had ever met, and I'd be a liar if I told you I hadn't thought about what it would be like to be with her. To hold her and look in her eyes when I was *inside her.*

But what we had was more than just the physical stuff. We talked for hours about pretty much everything. Music. Books. Family.

She told me about her brother. About the kind of kid he'd been, and for me, to be the guy she was willing to share all that stuff with was huge.

I felt like the king of the world, and for a while there, I felt like nothing could touch me. That's what this girl did for me.

But being a king and flying high meant that the fall could be epic. And in my case, epic didn't even come close.

It was Friday afternoon, and I'd come to town with my uncle to pick up a few things at the hardware store. We were nearly done with the gazebo but had run out of plywood trim for the base, and we needed to buy more paint.

Once we stored everything in the back of his truck, my uncle ran to the bank, and I walked a block down to the convenience store to grab us a couple of Cokes.

The girl behind the counter was someone I recognized, but I couldn't think of her name. Candy…Candace maybe? She was a year behind me in school, and I tried not to stare as she tugged her top down so that her boobs were nearly falling out. It was kinda hard not to. They were massive.

"Hey, Nathan. How's your summer going? I mean, I know it's probably hard and everything…and…"

I shrugged. "It's going."

I tossed a pack of gum on the counter to go along with my Cokes.

"I heard you and Rachel broke up."

I nodded but didn't answer. I didn't know the girl, not really, and it's not like we'd ever had a conversation before, so why the hell was she chatting me up about Rachel?

"I hear Trevor's the same. Not really improving. That's gotta be weird, you know? It's almost like he's stuck or something."

Annoyed, I ran my hand through my hair and rolled my shoulders. "I really don't know."

*And it's none of your business.*

The bell jingled behind me so I knew I wasn't the only one in the store anymore. I cleared my throat, a "let's get the freaking show on the road" kind of sound, but this girl was dense.

She rang up my order. "So, are you and Mrs. Blackwell's granddaughter like, you know, dating?"

Jesus. I handed over a five-dollar bill. I gave a noncommittal nod that she could take whatever way she wanted. Was she ever going to shut up?

"That's gotta suck," she said.

My head shot up, not really understanding her angle or her need to talk about my social life. "Why the hell do you care?" I said sharply.

Surprise widened her eyes and she stammered like an idiot. "You know, uh, because she doesn't live around here. I mean, she's going back to wherever it is she's from, isn't she? New York, I think someone said? And well, if you guys are together, then you won't really be together anymore and…"

Right.

"Thanks for pointing that out."

It's not like I hadn't thought about it every damn night for at least a week. Monroe's parents were coming in a few days and then…well, then she was going home and I had no idea how I was going to survive without her.

Pissed off, I grabbed my stuff from the counter and turned around without answering.

I turned around and nearly ran over Trevor's mom.

Holy. Shit. I wasn't ready for this.

She was even thinner than when I'd seen her at the hospital, and trust me, Trevor's mom was already skinny; she didn't need to lose weight. The purple dress she wore looked like it was two sizes too big.

Her eyes were sunken, kind of like the skin around them was too thin and bruised, and I glanced away because there's no way I could look into them. Jesus, it felt like someone had just punched me in the gut.

I couldn't see her pain. Not now.

My chest made this weird whooshing sound, like air had just been let out of a tire.

I think my heart stopped. Or maybe it was just the weird sensation of my stomach rolling end over end before falling all the way to the floor.

My fingertips started to tingle, and black dots flickered before my eyes.

"Nate, you don't look so good." Brenda Lewis watched me closely, her thin lips trembling, her hands running up and down her thighs nervously.

I couldn't answer. I couldn't say a damn thing, because my tongue was stuck at the back of my throat and those spots flickering in front of my eyes made it hard to concentrate.

"Shit," I said, shaking my head to try and stop the roaring in my ears. What the hell was wrong with me? "I'm sorry," I managed to say, though I wasn't sure she heard me. Or maybe the words had only echoed inside my head.

"Come with me," she said.

She touched me, her hand strangely cool and smooth on my skin, and I let her lead me out of the store.

I don't think my heart slowed down until we walked a few feet and stopped near a bench cemented into the sidewalk underneath an oak tree.

The shade wasn't dark enough and I wished that it were nighttime, because the shadows were thicker, easier to hide inside.

I didn't know what to do, so I popped open my Coke and took a sip, my eyes on the sidewalk, on the cracks that spread out like spidery fingers. The square I looked at was fractured. It was broken and in bad need of repair. Kind of like me.

Kind of like Trevor.

"Nate," she said softly. "Look at me."

*I can't.*

But I did.

"I've been calling your cell all morning."

What?

That bad feeling was back in a big way, and for a minute, I thought I was going to puke.

"Mrs. Lewis," I said weakly.

"It's Brenda," she answered gently. "It's always been Brenda."

I nodded and blew out a long, shuddering breath. I was so afraid to speak. To ask the question that hovered on the tip of my tongue.

"I forgot my cell at home," I said instead.

She nodded and wrapped her arms around herself, shivering as if she was cold. It was hot as hell, nearly 100 degrees, and yet I was the same. I felt like I'd been dipped into a bucket of ice.

"Your uncle told me you were in the store. I ran into him at the bank."

My heart spiked, pounding so fast and furious that, for a second, I was dizzy. I felt as if I'd just played the toughest football game of my life. As if I'd run every single play myself. Given everything that I had and it wasn't enough.

It would never be enough.

That bad feeling I'd had for weeks was back, worming its way through skin and bone and crushing a part of me that I didn't think would ever recover.

"I don't blame you, Nathan…for the accident. I know you would never do anything to hurt Trevor or anyone on purpose. You're a good boy. I want you to know that." Her voice was rough, but strong. "I know that Mike is being hard on you…he just…Trevor was his world, you know? And it's just so hard, and I…" A tear slipped down her cheek and she wiped it away, but another soon followed.

I didn't think I could feel any worse or sink any lower. But I guess I was wrong.

"I just wanted you to know that I don't blame you. I was a teenager once, and none of us were squeaky clean, especially Mike." She sighed. "I've done things that were stupid and thoughtless and dangerous." She shrugged. "All of us have."

"I don't…" I began and had to stop. "I don't know what to say, Brenda. I'm sorry doesn't cut it. It doesn't seem to be big enough."

"I know," she said softly.

For a few seconds, there was only silence between us, and I could see the expression on her face changing, as if she was gearing up to do something she really didn't want to do.

My teeth clenched, so tight that pain radiated along my jaw, but I didn't care. In that moment, all I saw was the fear and pain in Brenda Lewis's eyes. Fear and pain that I had put there, and no matter what she said, it didn't make me feel better.

Her fear filled me up, seeping into every nook and cranny, and for a second, I saw Monroe's face, and I wondered where she was. What was she doing at this exact moment?

Because if ever there was a moment that was going to crack my world wide open, this was it. I knew that my life was about to change again. I was coming down from the clouds and starting a free fall that would take me down hard.

No longer was I a king, flying high with Monroe. Nope, I was nothing but the pathetic excuse of a friend who had put Trevor in the hospital. I was nothing more than the sum of that night.

I saw all of that reflected in her eyes.

"Trevor took a turn for the worse overnight."

I shook my head. "No," I said hoarsely. "Oh God."

"Some sort of infection in his blood. His organs are shutting down. He's gone septic. There are some other issues, but…"

"Jesus." I stumbled a bit and she grabbed my elbow, steadying me against the stone bench.

"Mike and Taylor are with him now, but I know how much you love Trevor, and I think that you should come to the hospital tonight. I think that Trevor would want you there."

I stared at her in shock as she gently shook my arm and

then cupped my chin. There was nowhere to look but into her eyes.

"Do you understand what I'm telling you, Nathan?"

I nodded and said the hardest words I'd ever said in my life. "You want me to come and say good-bye. Say good-bye to Trevor."

Brenda Lewis let go of me and took a step back. She looked like a wounded animal. One who'd had its heart ripped out, and I guess I was responsible for that too. I felt the burden sitting on my shoulders, and God, I was so damn tired.

"Yes," she answered simply. "You might not get the chance again." Her voice caught and then she turned away.

I watched her shuffle down the sidewalk until she disappeared at the next block. When my uncle found me, I didn't have to say anything. I could tell he already knew.

I handed him his Coke and left him there.

## Chapter Twenty-Five
# Monroe

Gram found me on the porch, curled up on the settee, waiting for Nathan. He and his uncle hadn't come back after they'd gone into town for supplies earlier, but he usually showed up around now.

I was anxious to see him, which was crazy. I'd seen him at noon when I'd taken him a cold drink, but seriously, it felt like days since his smile turned my insides to mush. Days since he had kissed me until my head spun.

And now…now I sat and waited for a guy who had turned my world upside down. A guy who had finally fixed some of the broken pieces inside me. A guy I was going to say good-bye to soon.

With a sigh, I tucked a piece of hair behind my ear and pushed those thoughts away. I didn't want to think about the end of something so good. Not yet anyway.

It was dusk, that sweet spot just before evening fell, and the crickets chirped away, happy to play in the shadows now that the sun was gone.

I wore Nate's The Cramps T-shirt because I liked it and it smelled like him, which is what Gram caught me doing when she walked out onto the porch. Like a nerd, my nose was buried in the hem of his shirt and I let it fall, hoping she wouldn't notice the heat in my cheeks.

Gram walked over but stopped a few inches away, and as soon as I looked up, I knew something was wrong. Her eyes were sad, her mouth soft, and she had her hands clasped in front of her as if she didn't know what to do with them.

"Have you heard from Nathan?" she asked quietly.

My heart sank.

*Something was really wrong.*

"No." I shook my head and got to my feet. "What's going on? Is he okay?"

Gram watched me closely for a moment and then sighed. "Trevor Lewis has taken a turn, a bad turn, and the doctors don't know if he'll survive the night."

"Oh my God, Gram."

I fell back onto the settee and bent over, resting my hands on my knees as I stared at the floor. This was bad. Really bad. This would break Nathan.

"And Nathan knows?"

"Yes, but no one has seen him since this afternoon."

My head shot up at that. "What do you mean, no one has seen him? Wasn't he with his uncle?"

Gram nodded and sat down beside me, her warm arm around

my shoulders as she pulled me in tight. "He was, but he was upset when he learned the news and..."

"And what? His uncle thought it was okay to let him take off alone? Doesn't he know how screwed up Nathan's head is?" I jumped to my feet, my voice incredulous. "He blames himself, Gram, and that kind of hurt isn't good. That kind of hurt can make you do crazy things."

I slipped my feet back into my sneakers. "If Trevor dies..." My voice trailed off as I thought of Nate, and the fear inside me tripled.

"Do you think he would..." Gram paused, her hand over her mouth. "Do you think he would hurt himself?"

"No! I mean, I don't know." God, I hope not.

I thought back to the year before. To a time when I had a total disconnect from everyone. I knew what it felt like to think there was nothing...nothing that could make the pain go away.

And I knew how easy it was to consider a way out.

"I need to find him, Gram. Can I borrow the car?"

She nodded slowly and pulled the keys out of the pocket of her light gray sweater. "Take your cell phone. I'll let you know if he shows up here."

My mind was already racing ahead, wondering where he could be. I started down the steps, nearly falling on my face as I tripped over the last one, and I was halfway to the car before I pulled up cold.

My cell.

I whipped it out and called him, but after three rings it went to voicemail. I left a message asking him to text me or call me as soon as possible, and then I sent a text to Brent.

Have you heard from Nate?

He answered almost immediately.

No. You? The guys are worried. He's not picking up his cell.

Shit. I slid into the car.

**Me:** Let me know if you find him.
**Brent:** Will do. His car is missing.
**Me:** What? I thought he wasn't supposed to drive.
**Brent:** He's not. His parents are freaking out.

I stared at the flickering screen and sent one last text.

**Me:** Sorry to hear about Trevor.
**Brent:** It's so screwed up.

It was so much more than that. I gunned the car and hoped like heck Gram wasn't watching, because honestly, I barely missed her prized geraniums as I barreled down the driveway and headed for town.

It was the only place I knew to go, but once I got there, I wasn't exactly sure where to look. I drove past the fairgrounds where the Peach Festival had been held but it was empty. Nothing going on.

The baseball diamond next door was dark as was the football field behind the high school. I drove down Main Street and followed the signs to the hospital, retracing the route I'd taken only a few weeks earlier.

Weird. It felt so long ago. The festival. That first "non-date." How had he managed to mean so much to me in such a short time?

I thought that maybe I loved Nathan.

No. That was wrong. I didn't *think* anymore. I was sure of it.

I loved Nathan Everets, and I couldn't picture my tomorrow without him in it.

"Crap," I said aloud, glancing in my rearview mirror to make sure no one was behind me.

I had no idea if he would come to the hospital, but it was a place to start. I parked as best I could, considering I had to parallel-park Gram's giant-ass car, and two minutes later, I ran through the front doors.

Trevor was on the fifth floor, and when I got off the elevator, the lounge area near the nurses' station was empty. The whole place was quiet.

It smelled.

It smelled like pain and fear and death.

A walk around the nurses' station and a quick glance down each hallway that led from the main desk told me the place was deserted. More than a little nervous, I returned to the lounge, unsure what to do.

I sat on the old, worn vinyl sofa that I'd sat on before and shoved my hands underneath my legs for warmth, shivering when I heard someone cry out from down the hall. Was it a patient? Or a family member.

I guess it didn't matter, because either way, it meant that someone was in pain. Someone hurt, and that sucked.

A nurse at the station smiled at me. She looked young. Too young to be a nurse, but her pretty eyes and soft smile made me feel a little better. "Can I help you, hon? Visiting hours are nearly over."

I shook my head. "I should go," I said and jumped to my feet.

"Who are you here to see?" she asked.

"It's fine. No one."

I ran to the elevator, and once inside, pressed M for the main floor. The doors started to slide back into place but a large, meaty hand stopped them and a tall man stepped in with me.

I knew this man. I knew his tortured eyes. His large, powerful shoulders. The tattoos.

I recognized him from the last time I'd been here with Nathan. It was Trevor's dad.

And boy, did he look awful.

We rode down in silence, and I'm pretty sure he didn't even

know I was there. He was off somewhere, somewhere dark and sad, and when he stepped off, I followed.

I followed him out the front doors of the hospital and down the side until he stopped near a stone bench and a waterfall. I shivered slightly as I watched him pull out a cigarette and light it.

He took a long drag and leaned against the bench, head bent toward the starless sky as he slowly exhaled.

I watched him take another long drag. I stepped back, wishing the shadows were darker here. Why had I followed him? What was I doing? I needed to find Nathan, not stalk Trevor's dad.

"Do you know him?"

I jumped at the sound of his voice and glanced around quickly just to make sure he wasn't talking to someone else. But there was no one there.

Shit.

"No," I said carefully.

Trevor's dad glanced my way, and the unmistakable sheen of tears glistened on his face. He didn't try to wipe them. He just took another drag and flicked his ashes onto the ground.

"So why are you here?"

I stared back at him, unsure and more than a little intimidated by his size and his pain. I remembered how angry he'd been with Nathan. How he had threatened to kick Nathan's ass if he ever…

Panicked, I took a step closer.

"I'm looking for Nathan." The words tumbled from me before I could take them back, and I waited for his reaction, my gut churning with fear and my heart hurting at the pain in his eyes.

He didn't say anything. He just watched me for a few seconds and then took another drag before tossing his cigarette. Carefully he ground the butt with his booted foot and then pushed off from the bench.

He was too quiet, and suddenly I was more than a little scared—not for me, but for Nathan.

"Did you…did he come by? His parents are worried and I know that…" *I need to find him.*

He stopped a few inches from me, this large, powerfully built man. His hands were tight at his sides, fisted, and I took a step back.

"Who are you?"

Surprised, I didn't answer at first, and he shifted his feet, exhaling tiredly as he rolled his shoulders. The lines around his eyes deepened, sinking into his skin. I held my breath, not sure what to expect, but then he whispered, "Never mind."

He moved past me and I turned to watch him, unsure what I should do or say to make things right. I wanted to make things right. I wanted him not to hurt.

Everything about the man screamed pain. God, there was so much pain, and I was sick of it. It hung in the air, sucking up all the oxygen, making it hard to breathe.

It slid over me. *Into me.* And I stumbled, tears springing to my eyes at the unfairness of it all.

What had I, or Nathan, or this man done to deserve the crapton of hurt thrown our way? Had we pissed off the higher power? Had we done something so bad that we needed this heavy dose of pain to tip the scales back to where they were supposed to be?

Was it just our bad luck? Or was it fate?

Or maybe I had it all wrong. Maybe there wasn't a reason or a plan and I was overthinking everything. Maybe things just *were*, and the good and the bad happened for no reason other than *they just did.*

Stuff came at us, and it was up to each of us to handle it. Some of us survived and others, well, others just didn't. Maybe that was the point of it all.

But if you were like me, you survived because someone gave you a reason to.

"He's so sorry," I whispered. "You have no idea."

Trevor's dad stopped but didn't turn around, and I took that as a sign to keep going.

"Nathan would never hurt Trevor on purpose. The way he talks about him…it's like they're brothers or something, and it's killing him to know he made a mistake that put his best friend in the hospital."

My voice caught and I shuddered, cold and frustrated.

"I know that what happened to your son is the most awful thing ever—"

"You don't know shit, little girl."

I swallowed hard as Trevor's dad turned around and glared at me. "Who are you again?" he barked.

"Monroe. My name is Monroe Blackwell. I'm just a friend and…and you might not like to hear this, because I know that most adults don't like it when a kid tells them that, well, tells them that they're wrong." I paused and prayed for strength. "You're wrong."

He took a step closer, and that fear inside me expanded until I was trembling. But I didn't back down. I couldn't. I needed to make him understand. I needed to do this for the boy I loved.

"You're wrong to hate Nathan for what happened to your son," I gasped. "So, so wrong. It's not fair."

He made a sound—something almost inhuman—and took another step toward me. His eyes glistened with a hardness that made me flinch.

"Who the hell are you to preach to me about what's wrong or what's not fair? I'll tell you what's not fair. It's not fair that my son is lying in a hospital bed where he's been for over three months. It's not fair that now he's battling an infection that could kill him." He scrubbed at his eyes. "They think he's leaving us tonight, did you know that? The doctor told us this morning that they don't expect him to make it. Christ, Trevor isn't even seventeen. What in hell is fair about that?"

"Nothing," I whispered. "Nothing about this is fair, don't you see? What if Trevor had been driving that night and it was

Nathan in a coma? Would you think that your son deserved all this hatred? All this blame?"

"Trevor wasn't driving the damn car!" he roared.

"But he could have been." How could I make him see? "*He could have been!* We're kids. We make mistakes. We screw up and sometimes we screw up so badly that people get hurt. Haven't you ever done something so wrong or so bad that you wished you could take it back?"

*I have.*

My voice broke, and he looked away as I struggled to keep it together. "Look, we don't know each other and I've never met Trevor. But from what Nate told me, I think that, no," I shook my head, "no, I *know* that Trevor would hate what you're doing to his best friend. I know that Trevor would be big enough to forgive Nathan."

Tears shimmered in his eyes, and my heart turned over at the raw pain I saw there. "Forgive. That's a joke," he said hoarsely. "It's so damn hard."

I nodded. "I know. It's hard not to blame someone. It's hard to just accept when something awful happens because it hurts so much, but I…" I paused and choked back my own tears. "I don't think Trevor would want his best friend to be broken for the rest of his life. I think that Trevor would want his family to be compassionate. I think he would want them to forgive."

Trevor's father didn't say anything else. He looked away, stared at the ground for a few seconds, and then turned around.

He disappeared into the shadows, leaving only the sound of his footfalls to echo into the silence. To echo into my head.

And it seemed as if I stood there for forever, until the sound went away and I was able to move.

I turned in the opposite direction and let the shadows fall over me, but their darkness offered no relief. They only offered a window to disappear into—a moment in time—and I wondered if Nathan had found his own window. His own shadow.

And I wondered if it felt as empty as mine.

# Chapter Twenty-Six
## Monroe

It was close to midnight when I finally parked the Matlock in Gram's driveway. A light rain had started a few hours ago, and the temperature had gotten warmer instead of cooler. Thunder and lightning cut across the sky, but the rain remained steady, falling in soft waves against the windshield.

"Where are you, Nathan?" I asked the darkness, but of course there was no answer.

It felt like I had driven up and down every freaking street in Twin Oaks and then I'd headed to the drive-in, but there was no bush party tonight. I'd even swung by Baker's Landing, hoping that maybe he was there, but again it was quiet, with only the swans in the pond to greet me.

I was trying to be strong. Trying not to be mad at Nathan, but it was hard when I was basically going insane. I don't even know why I bothered coming back to Gram's—it's not like I was going to be able to sleep or anything—but I'd called her and told her I'd be home by midnight, and really, where else could I go? I didn't know where else to look.

I slipped out of the car and trudged toward the porch but paused, one foot on the bottom step, head to the sky as the rain slid over my cheeks. Somewhere in the darkness, I heard an owl. The sound was so lonely and sad. So freaking appropriate.

What was I doing? There was no way I could sleep.

I took a step back and then walked around the house. In the distance, the shadows were thicker, and my eyes moved over the large crypt where the family bones were buried.

Fireflies danced around the edge of the cemetery, appearing between the raindrops, only to disappear in a flash. And there just beyond the maze...*the maze.*

Oh my God, the maze!

I ran like a crazy person, nearly falling when my feet slipped in the wet grass, but didn't stop until I zigzagged through the familiar path and stopped in the center. Our center.

It was darker in here, the shadows falling from the six-foot-high hedge even thicker than outside, and with the rain sliding across my skin and into my eyes, at first I thought it was empty.

But then a shadow moved, there in the corner, and I held my breath, afraid that if I exhaled, my world would shatter and the vision would disappear. And I needed it not to disappear. I needed it to be real.

*Nathan.*

Gram told me once that there are moments that stay with us for the rest of our lives. Some of them are beautiful. Some are painful. And some don't seem to matter at all until much later.

But some, like this one, this moment about to happen, had the potential to be life-altering.

Nate scrubbed at his eyes, and that long hair of his was a mess of crazy waves that curled around his face and was plastered to his neck. His T-shirt clung to him, wet and transparent, his jeans equally soaked. Rain slid off him the same way it rolled off my skin, and as he stepped closer, I could see the pain in his eyes.

He hunched his shoulders forward and looked down at the ground. "I'm sorry," he said, his voice rough. "I drove until I couldn't drive anymore. I ditched my car down the road. I've been here for hours, but I didn't know what to do. What to say. So I just ignored everyone." He shuddered. "Even you."

Right now, here in this place that was ours, I didn't care about any of it. I only cared about him. About stopping his pain and helping him the way he'd helped me. Something fierce burned in my chest, something hot and wonderful and scary.

Something that maybe should wait, but I knew I wasn't strong enough to push it back. But was I strong enough to deal with the fallout?

"I love you," I whispered.

His head whipped up and he dragged his hand across his forehead, slicking his hair back out of his eyes.

"What?"

I took the steps that brought us so close I felt the heat radiating off him, and I placed my hands on his chest. I felt his heart beating. Heard the ragged breaths falling from his chest.

And I looked up into eyes that I could lose myself in.

"I know it probably sounds crazy to you. I mean, we just met not that long ago, but I love you, Nathan."

My hands slipped around his waist and I rested my head in the crook of his neck. *I love you.*

He shook against me, his body tense, and then his hands slid around my shoulders and he crushed me to him, his nose against my neck.

"I need you," he whispered. "So much. So damn much."

He jerked his head up, and then his hands were in my hair, tugging me until I was forced to look into his eyes.

"I love you, Monroe. God, I've never felt this way about a girl but…I just…there's so much shit and I don't know how to deal with it, and Trevor…he…"

Nathan rested his forehead against mine, and for a few moments, we breathed into each other.

For the first time in forever, I felt settled—which was crazy. And yet, it felt as if all the pieces of my life that had been moving, shifting, trying to find their way back, had finally clicked into place.

I was where I was supposed to be, and sure I was battered and had been beaten down, but I had made it through and I was whole. I was whole and I was alive and I was in love with a boy who wasn't quite there yet. A boy who had held my hand and gotten me to this place.

"I need you to not do this anymore, Nate. I need you to be strong, like you were for me, and I need you to forgive yourself."

"He could die," Nate whispered. "I knew it was a possibility, but I never thought…I thought he was going to wake up. I thought he was going to wake up and give me hell, you know? Hit me or yell at me or…something. I didn't think he would just…end."

"I know."

"I don't know what to do anymore. I'm so pissed off and angry and I hate myself for what I did to him. I go over that night. Over and over. I relive it, you know? And it drives me crazy because I can't remember the moment when it went wrong, and I don't know how to get past that."

"Let me help you, Nathan."

His voice broke. "How?"

Carefully, I pulled his hand into mine and stepped back. "Do you trust me?" Did I trust myself? When had I become the expert on healing? Me, the girl who had gone to therapy for over a year because I'd been so broken. The girl who had cut her wrists because she didn't want to deal.

And yet, as I looked into his eyes, I had such a feeling of *rightness* inside me that I was able to push back all the negative thoughts. The ones that said there was no hope. Only pain.

The ones that said I could lose Nathan if I wasn't careful.

I thought back to that day when I was eleven. To that hot afternoon on Gram's porch when she'd told me that I could do anything as long as I put my mind to it. And suddenly I knew she was right. She'd been right all along.

"I need you to trust me."

Nate said nothing.

"I need for you to let me catch you. Do you understand?" I touched his cheek again. Traced a line to his mouth and then stood on my toes so that I could kiss him. It was a gentle touch—a soft brush of the lips that cemented our connection.

"I won't let you fall," I whispered.

He nodded. It was enough.

"Okay," I said. "Let's go."

"Where?"

I swallowed my fear and tried to smile, though I wasn't sure it worked all that well. I knew we stood on the edge of a cliff, but I also felt like we could survive the fall.

We had to survive, or what was the point of it all?

"Let's go see Trevor."

# Chapter Twenty-Seven

# Nathan

The hospital was quiet when we arrived, with only a few cars in the parking lot and even fewer on the street outside. The rain had stopped, but the humidity hung in the air like a thick blanket, covering everything in gray mist.

Monroe slid into a parking spot behind a truck—the Lewises' truck—and that sick feeling in my gut churned hard. I didn't know if I had the balls to do this. I thought of the last time I had come here—of the anger that lived inside Trevor's dad—and despite Brenda's plea for me to come, I wasn't so sure he wouldn't kick my ass on sight.

Maybe it's what I wanted.

Maybe I'd let him.

My cell vibrated, and I yanked it from my jeans. It was a wonder the stupid thing still worked, considering it had been wet for hours.

It was my mom. I'd finally sent her a text letting her know I was all right and that I was with Monroe. I told her that I was going to the hospital and that I didn't know when I would be home. I glanced down to read her text.

I love you. So does Trevor.

Shit. My eyes burned again and I pocketed the cell, breathing out hard.

"Hey," Monroe said softly. "Are you ready?"

No.

"Yeah."

She leaned toward me and pressed her mouth to mine. It was just a soft touch, but I tasted the salt from her tears, the warmth of her soul, and the depth of her emotions. I felt that kiss all the way inside me where it settled next to my heart.

This girl had every part of me. Every single part.

"I'm glad you're here," I said, pulling back as that sick feeling heaved inside me again. "Because I don't think I could do this by myself."

She threaded her fingers through mine and squeezed my hand. "You're not alone, Nathan. Not anymore." She angled her head, her hair still wet and sticking to her neck. "I'd like to meet Trevor now."

She stared at me, her clothes wrinkled—my T-shirt two sizes too big—and I thought that she was the most perfect creature I'd ever seen.

"Trevor would have thought you were the coolest thing ever."

"I'm counting on it," she said slowly and then opened her door.

Less than five minutes later, we stood on the fifth floor, and the fear that had been dodging me all day was back, and it was back hard. I dropped Monroe's hand and shoved my own deep into the pockets of my jeans, avoiding the curious gazes from the nurses behind the station.

"Can I help you?"

The tall one came around the desk, eyebrows arched as she waited for us to answer.

"I…" Shit, my voice sounded worse than when I was twelve and it started to change. I cleared my throat, my gaze moving past the nurse to where Trevor's room was.

"Nathan's here to see his friend, Trevor Lewis," Monroe said.

The nurse's eyes narrowed, and she cocked her head, her eyes never leaving me. A moment passed. And then another.

My heart sank, because I saw the recognition in her eyes. She knew who I was. The screwup who was responsible for Trevor being here. There was no way she was going to let me walk past the damn desk.

What the hell had I been thinking?

"He *needs* to see Trevor," Monroe said forcefully. "You have to at least let him try."

"Honey, I don't need to do anything," the nurse replied, her hands now on her hips as if she'd made it her own personal mission to keep us away.

"Brenda..." I looked her in the eye. "Brenda Lewis, his mom, told me to come by when I saw her today. She said that he might..." I rolled my shoulders and tried to keep it cool. "She said that he might not make it 'til morning."

Shit. Hearing those words was tough; saying them was even tougher.

Something softened in her eyes and she sighed, shaking her head. "I'm sure she meant for you to come before nine. I'm sorry, but it's too late, and it's against hospital policy." She shook her head. "I'm going to have to ask the both of you to leave."

And that was it. Over before it could start.

"Are you kidding?" Monroe pushed past me, and for a second, I thought she might actually hurt the nurse. "Can't you see what this means to him? Trevor is his best friend. He *has* to see him. You have to let him."

The nurse shrugged. "I understand what you're saying, but we have rules and we have them for a reason, and if you don't leave quietly, I'll have to call security."

"Monroe, it's no use. Let's just go." I grabbed her elbow and would have turned except I heard a voice call my name, softly, but there was no mistaking the gruff undertone.

"Nathan."

I looked past the nurse and spied Mike Lewis standing just outside Trevor's room, and if it was possible for everything inside me to freeze, it did. My lungs. My heart. My brain. Everything stopped, like time was winding backward. I felt like

I was standing in ice, as if the blood rushing through my veins was frozen and slow.

The nurse was still chattering in my ear, though she'd moved a bit and I had nothing blocking my view. I had no idea what she was saying, because there was nothing but Mike in my vision. In my head.

Nothing but a slow blow to my heart.

Trev's dad looked as if he'd aged ten years since I had seen him. His skin was gray and his eyes, shit, his eyes were sunken, glassy, and so full of pain, I felt it like a physical blow.

As if he'd balled up those massive fists at his side and smashed them into my face.

For the longest time, he stared at me, those sad, angry, and haunted eyes pinning me hard. I wasn't sure what he was going to do. Was he going to finally kick my ass? Would that somehow make him feel better?

Because I gotta tell you that if it would, I'd gladly let him beat me. I'd let him lay his hands on me and get whatever relief he could. Anything to make his pain go away.

He pushed off from the wall and walked toward us, his gait slow. He was a big man, intimidating to most with his shaved head, tattoos, and massive shoulders. Yet when I looked at him, I saw the guy who took Trevor and me fishing every Friday after school when we were ten. The guy who helped us build go-karts and who rushed me to the emergency room when I broke my arm after an epic crash.

I saw the guy who let us play our loud ass music 'til all hours of the evening and who would watch us, bobbing his head even though I knew he'd rather listen to Big & Rich.

I saw the guy whose heart I had shattered.

He stopped a few inches away, his sleeveless wife-beater stained down the front of his chest—coffee maybe—and it was wrinkled, like he'd slept in it or grabbed it off the floor to come here.

He rolled his shoulders, his eyes never leaving me, but there was no danger in his voice when he spoke. He just sounded really tired.

"You look like shit, Everets."

I nodded. "I guess I do."

Mike ran his hand along at least a week's worth of stubble on his chin and his eyes slid to Monroe. "You again."

Wait. What? When the hell had they met?

I looked at Monroe, but she faced Mike Lewis, legs spread, arms at the ready as if… Hell, she looked like she was willing to fight him if she had to. And if it was possible for my heart to squeeze even tighter, it did.

That's what this girl did to me.

"Me again," she said softly.

"Mr. Lewis, I was just telling them it was too late for visiting hours." The nurse shifted on her feet, suddenly unsure.

Yeah, it was a long night, I got that, but I didn't care that she was tired of my shit. I didn't care about anything other than Trevor.

"I thought about what you said," Mike said gruffly, his gaze still on Monroe. "You were right."

I watched the two of them, not really understanding what was going on and wondering when the hell Monroe had hooked up with Trevor's dad.

"Thank you," Monroe said quietly.

"For what?" Mike answered.

"For being strong enough. For letting him in," Monroe replied.

Mike nodded abruptly and asked, "Can I have a moment with Nathan?"

"Actually, I've got to go," Monroe said softly.

My gaze swung from Trevor's dad back to Monroe. "What? No."

Dammit. I couldn't do this without her.

I reached for her but she ducked away, shaking her head, her soft eyes wide, their paleness shimmering beneath the harsh lights overhead.

"This isn't the place for me. Not right now." She hunched her shoulders. "Go. See your friend. Be with Trevor."

But I was shaking my head, suddenly so terrified my legs nearly buckled.

"You need to do this, Nathan, and when it's done, whatever happens, I'll be here for you."

I reached for her and she came, sliding her arms around my waist so that I could hold her for as long as she would let me.

It was enough. Touching her was enough.

In that moment, I felt like I could do anything.

I brushed my lips against her forehead and leaned close to her ear. "I love you."

Her hands clasped mine. "Ditto."

And then she was gone.

"She's special, that one," Mike said softly.

I nodded and turned, making no effort to hide the pain and remorse and anything else that was inside me.

"Mr. Lewis," I said, but he interrupted me.

"It's Mike. It's always been Mike."

I had to clear my throat several times before I could speak again. I felt tears pricking the corners of my eyes, and it took everything inside me to keep them away. In the end, it didn't matter, and I scrubbed at my eyes and exhaled loudly.

I couldn't remember a time when my body wasn't tight. Couldn't remember a time when there wasn't pain. Sure, I knew it was back there—back before that night—but as I stood in front of Trevor's dad, I thought that I would never remember what it was like before then, no matter how hard I tried.

"How is he?" I asked carefully, forcing the words out one at a time.

I held my breath, afraid I'd been too late and that my worst nightmare was about to become a reality.

Mike clasped me on the shoulders but I still couldn't look up at him. I was too afraid. Too much of a coward. I felt his forgiveness. Felt it wrap around me like a spider's web, and yet…

I still couldn't shake the feeling that I didn't deserve it and I wasn't strong enough to face this reality if Trevor wasn't going to be in it.

So I stared at my muddied boots and prayed like I've never prayed before.

"He's still with us."

The air whooshed out of me so quickly that if Mike's hands hadn't have been on me, I would have fallen on my ass.

"I brought his guitar, you know. Thought maybe music would help him fight this infection. Maybe music would bring him back, but…" He sucked in a breath and paused.

Slowly I looked up. "But?"

A sad smile touched his mouth. "I suck, remember? I only know a couple of chords, and G and C don't really cut it."

His smile widened and then he laughed. He laughed so hard that his body shook and his fingers dug into my shoulders painfully. I wasn't sure if he was going crazy or if he was just so tired he didn't know what he was doing.

He stopped abruptly and squared his shoulders. "I'm sorry, for the way I was after the accident. It was wrong to put all the blame on you and I…I have no excuse other than I was in a goddamn black hole and I needed someone to hit. It was you." He cleared his throat. "There was only you."

"It's okay," I said quietly.

And it was.

"Would you play for him? I mean, I think it might help. Maybe spark something inside him."

I couldn't answer. There was no way I was getting any words out. But I nodded. I nodded like a goddamn bobble head and followed Mike Lewis back down the hall.

# Chapter Twenty-Eight
## Monroe

I was dreaming about Malcolm. It was summer. Hot and humid with air so thick you could practically see it.

It was the kind of day when the pavement burned right through your sandals. The kind of day you'd spend hours running through the sprinklers at the water park. It was the kind of day when everything is slow and lethargic.

It was the kind of day when bad things happened.

I'd had this dream before, and it always ended the same. I lost Malcolm, there in the shadows, the deep ones that the sun didn't seem able to find.

I lost him, and usually I heard him crying for me. For Mom. For Dad.

The sound drove me insane, but this time…this time there was no crying. For a while, there was nothing—I knew he was gone but there was just nothing.

Then I heard his laughter riding the air like bubbles falling over a waterfall. They were light, dancing in the air. Clear, round sparkles that filled my chest until I couldn't breathe.

"Malcolm," I whispered, afraid that the sound would go away. God, I didn't ever want it to go away.

But it did.

His giggles faded until I couldn't hear them anymore, and no matter how much I tried to find them…to find that slice of time where he existed, I lost him.

I lost him in the sunlight and the water and the endless heat.

• • •

I woke abruptly and lay in my bed for a good ten minutes, just remembering how he sounded. How he smelled. How he felt.

My skin was drenched in sweat, and I was still in the clothes I'd worn the day before. My hair looked like it hadn't been combed for days, and I groaned. Ugh. I needed a shower.

Sunlight poured into my room, and the clock on the dresser across from me told me that it was nearly noon. I grabbed my cell but there were no messages from Nathan. I guess that was a good thing. In this case, no news was good news.

The hot water felt like heaven, but the restlessness in me had me showering as if I was running a race, and less than ten minutes later, I was trudging down the stairs, wet hair leaving streaks down my green sundress as I took them two at a time.

Eager to get back to the hospital and Nathan, I rounded the bottom step but froze when I heard voices from Gram's kitchen.

For a second, I wanted to run back upstairs and turn back the clock, because I knew that, for me, summer was almost over.

And that meant no more Nathan.

Pain twisted inside my chest at the thought of what Labor Day weekend meant, but I forced myself to take those steps until I leaned against the doorframe and watched Gram chatting with my mother.

Instead of her usual business clothes—Mom was a lawyer in Manhattan—she was dressed in a simple white T-shirt and a pair of blue-and-white plaid shorts. Her golden hair, normally kept in a sleek, straight cut to her jaw, touched the tops of her shoulders. She'd left it natural, and the waves looked incredible on her.

She was still too skinny, but it was nice to see her looking relaxed. Kind of normal. I suppose it was all we could hope for.

*Kind of normal.*

Dad leaned against the counter by the sink, watching his mother—Gram—as she talked up Mom. He was casual too, wearing an old pair of jeans and a Rolling Stones T-shirt. There was a lot more gray in his hair, and he had lost weight as well, but he looked good.

They both looked good, all things considered.

Just then, my dad glanced up and my heart turned over as he stared at me in silence, Gram and Mom still talked softly, unaware that I was there.

In that moment, I saw the love, the pain, the anguish, and the question…was I better?

Was I?

Were they?

For so long, he'd acted as if our small, battered family had already moved on. As if the tragedy that had happened to Malcolm had been dealt with—wrapped up in an ugly box and put into storage. It used to piss me off so much. How could he *not* wallow in the pain? Pain is what made us remember.

But I think I kind of got it now. It was how he'd been trying to deal with the fact that his son was gone, and even though his daughter was still around, she'd pretty much taken a vacation. I had been nothing after Malcolm died.

Just skin over a bunch of bones with no heart and no soul.

I'd been so wrapped up in my own pain that I hadn't once considered my parents didn't know how to deal with theirs.

I'd thought that Dad's apathy and Mom's need to overcompensate in everything was their way of dealing with me. But it wasn't. God, it wasn't at all. It was them falling away and trying to deal with their own pain.

The thing was?

We were still here. My mom. My dad. My gram.

*Me.*

*I was still here.*

I thought of the dream I'd had less than an hour ago, and I realized something. Even though Malcolm was dead, he wasn't *gone*. Not really.

He existed inside each and every one of us, in that one place

234

where he'd never left. That one piece of my soul that hadn't faded to black like the rest of me.

Malcolm had never really left us; it was me who had gone away. Me who had crawled deep inside myself because I wasn't strong enough to deal with everything. But Malcolm? He was still here with us.

I saw his hazel eyes reflected in my dad's. I saw his gentle, curious smile appear on my mom's face as she nodded at something Gram was saying.

Malcolm would always be here.

My feet started moving before I even knew what I was going to do and I didn't stop until his arms encircled me. Until I was breathing in that scent that was all Dad—part soap and musky cologne and just…just Dad.

When was the last time I'd let him touch me? The last time I'd given him a hug or a kiss? I couldn't remember, and I thought that, that alone was tragic. He used to be my king, back when I was little, and when had all of that fallen away?

Finally his hands slipped away and I took a step back, my gaze sliding from him to Mom.

"I missed you guys."

Mom didn't look like she knew what to say, and I could see tears sparkling around the corners of her eyes. She still sat at the table with Gram, who squeezed her hand and slowly rose.

"Monroe, why don't you grab the iced tea off the counter and pour us each a glass?"

"Sure, Gram."

I bent low and kissed my mom's cheek, but then quickly crossed the kitchen before she said anything. Our relationship had always been more complicated, and things were still fragile.

But the road back to good, though fragile, wasn't one I was scared of anymore.

I poured four iced teas and leaned against the counter sipping mine while Gram served peach cobbler. I hadn't had breakfast yet, but the thought of food—any kind of food—made my stomach turn.

"Nathan hasn't called, has he?" I finally asked when I couldn't stand it anymore. My cell still showed no calls or text messages, and I thought maybe he'd called the house.

Gram shook her head. "No, dear. I haven't heard anything."

"Who's Nathan?" Dad asked, sitting a little straighter in his chair as he fingered his glass.

*The boy that I love.*

Just then, a loud rap sounded on the back door that Nate always used and my heart nearly beat out of my chest as I watched it slowly open.

Nathan strode into the kitchen, his tall, lean form still in the wrinkled, dirty clothes he'd worn the day before. He hadn't shaved in a few days, and his jaw was shadowed while his hair was a wild mess—a hot, sexy, wild mess that haloed his head in burnished waves.

Burnished waves that I wanted to touch.

He pulled up short and my heart turned over when I saw how tired he looked.

"Hey," I said softly.

He held my gaze for several, long seconds and then attempted a smile. "Hey." Shoving his hands into the front of his jeans, he slowly looked around the room.

"Nathan," Gram interrupted, "you look exhausted. Have you eaten?"

He shook his head. "I'm not really hungry, thanks, Mrs. Blackwell."

He glanced around the room and cleared his throat. "I didn't know you had company." And then he turned. "I should go."

I sprang forward. "Nathan, no. Wait."

I was at his side in an instant, my hands reaching for him. Needing him. And when I slid my arms around his waist, I felt his muscles release and he sagged against me.

It was as if we were the only two people in the room. Heck, in the entire universe. He was all I was aware of and I glanced up at him, eyes searching, needing to know.

And like we were a part of each other, I didn't have to ask.

"He made it through the night and they think…" Nathan blew out a long breath. "They think that he's going to beat the infection."

"Oh my God, Nate."

"I know," he murmured into my hair. "He's still not out of the woods, but the doctor seems hopeful. I had to see you before I went home. Came straight here. I just had to…hold you."

A throat cleared behind us and Nathan shifted a bit, smiling down at me as he raised his eyebrows.

"Those your folks?"

I nodded. "Yeah."

"I guess I don't exactly look presentable."

"You look perfect," I answered and then nudged him with my hip. "Even though you look like crap." I paused. "Would you like to meet them?"

He tucked a piece of my hair behind my ears and stood back, and I don't think my heart could feel any more full. It was full of life. Full of love and family.

It was full of Nathan.

"Sure."

"Okay," I teased. "But don't say I didn't warn you." My hand slid down to his and I tugged him forward.

"Warn me?"

I nodded. "Yep. Both of my parents are lawyers and they kind of, you know, like to ask a lot of questions."

"Good to know," he said softly. "Let's do this."

# Chapter Twenty-Nine

# Nathan

Labor Day weekend. Where the hell did you come from?

Man, it didn't seem that long ago when summer felt as if it was as long as a school year. Back then, my life had been divided into two things. School. And summer. And in my young little mind, each was like a season, as long as each other.

When I was in elementary school, I hated Labor Day weekend because it meant no more lazy summer days spent out at my grandparents' place. No more afternoons in the pond at Baker's Landing, fishing or frogging. It was back to the classroom, and who the heck wanted to spend every day inside?

Not me. I'd rather be exploring, pretending to be the meanest pirate this side of the Mississippi.

But as I got older, went through middle school and then into high school, things changed. Traditions formed, and Labor Day weekend became a three-day celebration of not only the end of summer, but the beginning of another school year.

There was the annual football game. Fathers against sons.

And then there was the annual blowout bush party, held at a different location each year. It was a music- and booze-fueled night of mayhem, good times, and making memories.

This year, my senior year, would have been epic. *Would have* being the choice words.

Trevor was still in the hospital, and though his body had responded to the drugs and he'd fought off the infection that had basically shut down his organs, he was still in a coma. Still existing somewhere other than here, and I had no idea if he was gonna make it.

He wouldn't be starting senior year with me. Wouldn't be catching my throws on the football field or gigging at local clubs. And tomorrow…shit, tomorrow Monroe was flying home to New York City.

"Everets, your arm is looking damn good!"

I turned as my coach, Mr. Forster, jogged over from the other side of the field. We'd just finished playing against the fathers and I had thrown for a win by twenty-one points. Wasn't hard to do. They had a few players with some legs—my dad was one of them—but for the most part, they were a bunch of overweight, middle-aged guys who were already searching for the beer tent.

Coach Forster knocked his hat back and planted his hands on his hips. "Should be a good year."

"Yeah, I guess."

Truthfully, I wasn't all that interested in playing ball. Wasn't all that interested in much, but I'd made a promise to Monroe and I planned on keeping it. I had to be positive for her. Positive for myself.

"We'll miss Trevor for sure, but I've got my eye on that young Caleb Obinksky."

"Yeah," I said. "Sure."

I didn't give a shit about Caleb Obinksky. Where the hell was Monroe?

"Look, coach, I gotta go. Hit the showers."

Mr. Forster grinned, slapped me on the back, and then paused to shake my hand. "I just want to say that all that stuff..." He cleared his throat.

"Stuff?"

"The stuff with Trevor. It's in the past. New year. New outlook."

I didn't know what to say, because his analysis of the situation was so far off my grid that I couldn't see it. He wanted a winning season.

I just wanted to get by.

And I didn't ever want to forget what happened that night, because to forget meant that it could happen again. And I was never going to be so goddamn selfish and stupid. Never.

"Sure. Okay."

I pushed past him, my gaze roaming over the field until I saw that familiar dark head. She was chatting with Brent and a few others, her parents several feet away with her grandmother.

I jogged across the field, my eyes only on her, and I lifted my chin when she looked up. My heart did that strange flipping thing—was I ever going to get used to it? And I pushed Brent out of the way so that I could get to her.

"Hey! What the fu—" Brent stalled when Mrs. Blackwell arched an eyebrow, and he punched me in the arm. "You could have asked me to move, douche bag."

"Whatever."

I bent down and kissed her nose, inhaling that summery scent that was all Monroe. My forehead rested on hers, and I hoped she didn't mind that I was filthy and sweaty because I didn't want to move.

"Hey," I said.

She laughed and slid her hands up my arms until they hit my shoulders. "You're really good, Nate. Wow. I mean, I knew you would be, but I couldn't take my eyes off you."

I grinned. "Good, because I was showing off for you. Look, I gotta go home and shower. Brent's gonna pick me up later and we'll head out to the party. Sound good?"

"Sounds great."

She bit her lip in that adorable way that made me crazy, and I swear if it weren't for her parents watching us like hawks, I would have slipped my tongue inside her mouth and kissed her senseless.

But I had to be good. Her parents weren't 100 percent sure of me and I got that, but I didn't want anything to interfere with our plans. Tonight was our last one together, and I had to make it count. I needed to make this girl so crazy about me she would never forget this summer, or me.

Because I knew I wouldn't. She was burned into my skin like a tattoo, and I would carry her with me forever.

# Chapter Thirty

# Monroe

I changed my clothes at least seven times before settling on a pair of dark navy skinny jeans, ballet slippers, and a green halter top that made my eyes pop. Or at least that's what the saleslady said when Gram had taken me shopping in New Orleans a few weeks back.

The top was on the skimpy side—most of my stomach was bare and the jeans rode low—but I couldn't wait for Nate to see me. I had plans for tonight. For me and him.

I grabbed my purse from the table beside my bed and fumbled inside the hidden pocket until my fingers closed around the small foil packet.

I'd bought condoms when I was in New Orleans. My cheeks burned at the thought—I still couldn't believe I'd had enough balls to do it. It had been hard, slipping away from Gram, and then, well, who knew there were so many different kinds? Ribbed. Glow in the dark. Stuff that vibrated.

God, there were different sizes!

I'd bought the plainest, smallest box I could find and prayed that Gram wouldn't be able to tell. You know, in case there was some invisible sign on my forehead that said, *"Monroe is going to have sex and she has a box of condoms in her bag."*

I'd been thinking about this for days. No. Weeks. I'd been thinking about it ever since Nathan had kissed me at Baker's Landing. And tonight was my last chance. My last chance to be with Nathan. Really be with Nathan.

Outside, there in the maze that was ours, we'd spent most nights under the stars until he had to go home. We'd kissed. A lot. And we'd touched. I'd explored his hard, muscled body that was so different from mine, and he'd kissed his way down my chest, but he'd always held back, didn't go further. And when I wanted to do more, he stopped us.

Said we needed to move slow. That *he* needed to move slow.

So I hadn't touched him. Or seen him there.

Even though I'd wanted to.

I knew that Nate had had sex before. I'd asked him and he'd been honest with me. He'd told me that he and Rachel had been doing it since the tenth grade. When I pushed him, he'd admitted that there had been others.

Of course there had been others. Nathan Everets was hot. And it wasn't just that physically he was smoking. He was the deepest, sweetest guy I'd ever met. Who wouldn't want to be with him?

So why didn't he want me?

I shoved the condom into the front pocket of my jeans and glanced at myself in the mirror. For a moment, I didn't recognize the face that stared back at me.

Who was this girl with eyes that sparkled and skin that glowed? This girl who looked…happy. Excited. And scared.

"Monroe, Nathan is here!"

Gram's voice made me jump, and I grabbed my jean jacket. I shut the door and didn't stop until I was at the front door when I nearly tripped over my feet.

Holy. Hell.

Nathan smiled, a slow, soft grin that could seriously melt anyone's heart. His eyes were soft and I noticed that he'd shaved. I loved it when he didn't shave—it gave him that edge that I really liked—but tonight, with that smile? My hands were itching to touch all that smooth, tanned skin.

He wore a plain white Henley, his golden skin and burnished hair a contrast that could make any girl lose her head and—I smiled—he wore my favorite jeans. They were old and faded, but they looked amazing on him, and I exhaled shakily as I snuck a look at my mom.

She leaned against the staircase, and I could tell that Nate's charm was working overtime because she smiled at him. She smiled at him in a way I recognized. God, he was good.

"So," she cleared her throat. "You kids won't be too late?"

"Mom, it's my last night here, and I promise I won't be out all night, but can I stay out later than midnight?"

I saw the indecision in her eyes.

"I mean, I just haven't felt so good about things in so long, I kinda want to hold on to it as long as I can, you know?"

Okay, that was low, but I didn't care. I was willing to work any angle in order to spend as much time with Nathan as I could.

"I promise, I'll be good."

Gram and Dad walked up from the kitchen. "You take care of my granddaughter, Nathan."

"Yes, ma'am," he answered.

I gave my mom a quick hug, but she held me for a second longer. "Roe," she said shakily. "I…"

There were so many words between us. Simple words. Hard words.

It's the in-between words that are easy to get out. I guess, somehow, they don't really matter. They fill in the spaces between the simple ones that carry so much weight and the hard ones that hold everything together.

But the ones that do matter, those ones are the hardest to get out. They get stuck, or buried, and sometimes they get forgotten. But I knew they were there inside my mom, because the same ones were buried deep in me.

Mom shuddered and I whispered, "I know."

She paused. "You look beautiful."

I smiled at my dad and kissed Gram on the cheek. She grabbed my hands, her eyes suddenly serious as she bent forward. "Be careful," she whispered, so low only I could hear, her eyes full of meaning.

God. It's as if she knew what I was planning.

I nodded, my throat tight, and then followed Nate out into the hot Louisiana night.

The party was huge. It was held in the bush out back at some guy Chad's farm, and there must have been at least two hundred kids there when we arrived.

That was over two hours ago, and I'd bet there was close to three hundred by now.

A bonfire burned brightly, tunes blared from large speakers set on top of a mud-splattered redneck truck, and everyone seemed to be either high on life or high on weed, but sometimes it was hard to figure out the difference.

"Hey," Nate slid his arms around me and I leaned back against him, watching Brent chat up yet another girl.

"Is he, like, the biggest ho around?"

Nate laughed, his breath warm against my neck. "He's leaning that way."

Warm tingles spread down my body and that restless feeling was back. "Can we get out of here?" I asked softly, turning so that I could see him.

Nate's eyes were intense as he gazed down at me, and in that moment, if felt like we were the only ones around for miles. The music, the noise, and the kids—they all disappeared into the dark. There was just us.

"It's our last night and I just…I want to be alone with you."

Nate pulled me close and rested his chin on top of my head. His heart beat fast beneath my fingers, and I knew he was in the same place I was. It wasn't a place of in-between. It was hot and edgy.

I squeezed my eyes shut and burrowed deeper into his embrace. God, I wanted to crawl inside him. I'd never felt like this before, but then again, I'd never loved. Not like this.

"My parents," he said haltingly. "They're gone overnight. A friend's houseboat on the river."

My eyes flew open and I whispered, "So there's no one at your house?"

A pause.

"No."

I yanked my head back. "Let's go," I whispered, my hand falling to his.

He smiled then, a soft sort of thing that would make anyone fall harder. "I can't drive."

"But I can." I tugged him again, and this time he laughed out loud. Which, I gotta say, kind of pissed me off.

"You didn't drive to the party."

"I know." I let his hand drop. "Hold on."

"Where are you going?"

"You'll see."

My insides were on fire. No. No, they weren't. They were cold and shivery, and I kind of felt sick and excited all at once. I spotted Brent on the other side of the bonfire, his hand in some girl's hair, his mouth on hers.

I walked around a large group of kids and was nearly to him when Rachel stepped in front of me. I'd seen her earlier; it was hard not to—she was dressed in the skimpiest pair of shorts I'd ever seen and a bikini top that barely covered her impressive boobs. There were hickeys on her neck, her makeup was smudged, and she smelled like cigarettes.

She was a mess. I wasn't sure if she was drunk or high or both, but something was going on.

I wanted to hate her, but there was something almost desperate in her eyes, and the way she stared at Nathan told me a lot. She still loved him. She still wanted him.

"Can I talk to you?" she asked, unsteady on her feet as she jerked her head to the left.

I was surprised. Other than when she'd shoved a mental knife in my back that night at the Coffee House, we'd not said one word to each other.

"I…"

Shit. Brent was making his move and melting into the shadows. I needed to get his keys before—

"Please?"

I glanced back toward Nathan, but he was talking up some huge guy with massive shoulders. Football was written all over him.

Rachel took a sip of the beer in her hand and then tossed

it, but her eyes never left me. What did she want? Did I want to know?

"Sure," I said and followed Rachel past the line of trees on this side of the clearing. She stopped a few feet in, her back to me, and it took a few seconds for me to realize that she was crying. Her shoulders shook and a sob echoed into the night.

I wasn't sure what to do and, honestly, was about to take off, when she turned around so fast, she nearly fell.

Feeling weird about all of this, I took a step back.

She sniffled loudly. "Nathan's a good guy." Her voice broke and she wiped her hand under her nose, shoulders hunched as she looked at me from behind her raccoon-like eyes.

I didn't know what to say so I stayed silent.

"I miss him, you know? But it's over between us." She wrapped her arms around her body and shook her head. "I think it was over before that night."

I didn't get it. "Why are you telling me this?"

Rachel smiled, a sad sort of smile that never reached her eyes. She shrugged. "I don't know why." She looked down at the ground. "He was going to break up with me that night. Bailey told me. So I kept feeding him beers whenever I got the chance. Anything to keep him from telling me we were over."

When she glanced back at me, I saw the same pain in her eyes that I saw in Nathan's.

"I'm just as much to blame as Nathan is for what happened that night."

"Maybe you should tell him that," I whispered.

She shoved her hands behind her back and sighed. "Maybe." She paused. "I hear you're heading back to New York City tomorrow."

I nodded.

"Nathan's a good guy. I'm glad he found some kind of peace with you."

"Thanks," I mumbled, not really knowing how to respond to that. So I kept it simple. "Have a good…night," I managed to say.

Abruptly I turned and plowed through the trees until I made it back to the clearing. I spied Brent almost immediately, there near the edge with his girl, and I ran to him.

"Can I borrow your car?"

Brent glanced up, his mouth still on the girl's neck, a slow grin on his face as he licked her once and then turned to me. "You and Nate want some alone time?"

I nodded, not in the mood to play games, as I held out my hand.

He reached into his front pockets and then tossed the keys to me. "I'll get a ride with someone."

"Thanks."

In seconds, I was back with Nathan, and I guess I looked wild or crazy or, I don't know how I looked, but he waved off *football buddy* and grabbed my hand.

"Are you all right?"

I nodded. "Yeah."

*No.*

"Can we get out of here?"

Nathan stared down at the keys in my hand. "Are you sure about this?"

I reached up and kissed his mouth, this boy who I loved so much, and I whispered, "I've never been more sure about anything."

His dark eyes fell to my lips and he nodded. "Okay."

"Okay," I repeated, pulling him after me as we disappeared into the dark.

# Chapter Thirty-One
# Nathan

The ride back to my place didn't take long. Five minutes maybe. But it was a long five minutes.

A long five minutes filled with a lot of thoughts I wasn't so sure I should be thinking about.

First off, Monroe looked so freaking hot tonight that I'd barely been able to keep my hands off her. That little top she wore had Brent's eyes bugging out of his head when he'd first laid eyes on her.

I couldn't blame the guy. He was human, after all, but still. I'd never felt this possessive of a girl before, and when I caught Chad checking her out—elbowing the guys on the team to do the same—I could have easily gone all caveman on them, but I didn't think Monroe would like that kind of shit.

But the thing that made all of this so much harder was the fact that this was our last night together, and though I tried to keep my thoughts PG, it hadn't exactly worked.

I thought about her in that little bikini she'd worn when I

had taken her to Baker's Landing. I thought of how she'd felt all slippery and wet. How her pupils dilated when she kissed me and she made these sounds in her throat when I kissed her back.

She was so beautiful. So damn perfect.

And I didn't know what to do with that. It wasn't that I didn't think I deserved her, I was over that shit. But I loved this girl—I loved her more than I thought it was possible to love a girl. And here we were, counting down our last minutes together, and I suppose I should have been happy to just cuddle and talk, but man, all I could think about was getting her alone. In my room.

Naked.

"We're here."

Yanked from my thoughts, I glanced at my house. A house that was in darkness.

A house that was empty.

She cut the engine and turned to me. "I had to get out of there," she said suddenly.

"I know." I tried to make things light, but when she turned to me, there were tears in her eyes. What the hell?

"Hey," I whispered, unbuckling my seat belt as she did the same and scooted over onto my lap. "What's wrong?"

She shook her head as if she was trying to decide what to say, and then she spoke so softly I had to listen hard in order to hear her.

"I talked to Rachel."

"Rachel," I repeated.

I tried to keep it together. To keep it cool. But the truth was, there was a lot that Rachel could tell Monroe if she wanted to screw my night up. *A lot.* Shit. This had to be a guy's worst nightmare. No one wanted their ex-girlfriend gossiping about sex stuff to the new girlfriend.

"She seems really messed up."

I nodded. Messed up was an understatement. I'd known Rachel for a long time, and she was way more messed up than anyone knew. There were a lot of family issues—mainly with her stepfather—and she smoked too much weed and drank more than she should. I wasn't sure if she was ever going to be the carefree fun girl I started dating in ninth grade.

"What did she want?" I asked hesitantly.

"I'm not sure," Monroe said. "But I think she was checking to make sure I was treating you right."

Huh.

Monroe was quiet for a few moments, her forehead furrowed as if she was thinking really hard.

"She's going to need someone this year. I mean, I won't be upset if you are the one she leans on."

"So let me get this straight. You're giving me permission to hang out with my ex-girlfriend."

Her eyebrow rose. "Just hang out. You know, if you want to, because I think she needs someone right now."

God, I loved this girl.

"But no touching," she continued.

I grabbed her chin. I stared into her eyes so she had to see me—had to know how I felt. "I don't want to touch anyone but you, Monroe. There is no one else for me." I shrugged. "There just isn't."

"Let's go inside."

I knew what she was asking. What she wanted. And it's not like I hadn't thought about it every night for the past few weeks. It's not like I hadn't dreamed of being with her. Of watching her breathe and move. Of knowing what it felt like to be inside her.

But…this wasn't just any girl. "Are you sure, Monroe?"

Her lips slid across mine until her mouth was against my ear. "Yes."

• • •

The house was in darkness but she didn't care.

"Where's your bedroom?"

I grabbed Monroe's hand and led her down the hall. My room was at the back of the house, and I shoved the door open, following Monroe inside.

"Is there a light?" she asked, her voice light like a whisper on the wind.

I crossed to my bed and turned on the lamp. Its glow was muted, which was nice, and I watched the shadows that danced across her face.

She twirled a piece of hair between her fingers and I knew her well enough now to know that she was nervous. Hell, so was I. I'd never had sex with someone who I was in love with, and it mattered so much more on so many levels.

Sure, I thought I'd been in love with Rachel, but now I knew different. Now I'd felt and touched real love. Real love was full of emotion—it wasn't just about the physical stuff, getting laid or making out.

Emotion and love together? It changed things.

"I've never…" Her eyes slid away from mine. "I've never done it before."

I'd suspected Monroe was a virgin, and the enormity of what she was giving me pressed into my chest and I ran my hands through my hair, because in that moment, I didn't know what to do.

"I'm sorry. I should have told you." She sounded anxious. Scared.

I took the two steps needed to reach her and slid my hands into her hair, holding her so that there was nowhere for her to look but at me.

"God, Monroe. Don't apologize. Don't apologize for being you. For being the most incredible girl I've ever met." She was everything to me. "I love you."

"Then kiss me," she said softly, standing on her toes to reach me.

I kissed her for the longest time. Holding her softness against me as my head spun crazily and my heart tried like hell to keep up.

Things got heavy. They got wicked heavy.

We were on my bed. My T-shirt was on the floor.

Monroe felt so damn good, and when she rolled over on top of me, I was nearly out of my mind. Her long hair was all over the place, her pale skin smooth in the dim light. Her mouth was swollen from my kisses, her cheeks flushed and rosy.

She was the hottest thing I'd ever seen, and when she slowly reached behind her neck, I froze.

We were both breathing pretty hard by this point, and I couldn't look away as she undid her halter top and slowly peeled it away.

Nothing but my ragged breaths filled the air.

She straddled me and moved her hips slightly and I groaned. "Jesus, Monroe."

I couldn't take my eyes off her, and when she bent forward to lie against me, to press her softness into me, I think I might have died a little.

My hands crept up her bare back and I held her there, fighting for some kind of control.

I banged my head back into the pillow and swore under my breath.

"Nate?" she whispered into my neck. "Don't stop."

I turned my head and grimaced, fighting for some kind of control because things were moving fast and she felt way too damn good in my arms.

"Nate? Don't you want…me?"

I inhaled a deep breath and reached for her, cupping her jaw so that I could stare into her eyes. I didn't say anything. My mind was searching for the right words, so for a long time, I held her. I held her until her breathing slowed, and eventually, so did mine.

"Tell me it's not just me who feels this connection," I finally said, needing to hear her say the words.

"No," she whispered. "It's not just you, Nate."

"Have you felt like this before?"

She shook her head no but didn't answer.

"This connection that we have, Monroe. It's not like anything I've ever felt before." I had to try to make her understand. "And we have to work to keep it strong. Things are going to be tough with you back in New York, but we can make it work."

"Okay…"

"No, I need you to listen. There is no okay. There is no right or wrong here. I don't want to do anything to make you regret me. To make you regret us."

"I could never regret us. I want this, Nate. I want to know what it feels like to belong to someone. To belong to you. In every way possible."

God, to hear her say those words.

I searched her face. I looked into her eyes until my own blurred and I couldn't see shit.

"Are you sure that you want to…"

But her mouth was on mine and there were no more words.

There was only the taste of her lips, the feel of her tongue, and her body against mine. Hands seeking and legs entwined.

I held her as long as I could before I thought I was going to explode, and when she finally moved onto her back and reached for me, I was done for. I wanted her and I wanted to be her first.

As corny as it sounded, I wanted to be her only guy.

But most of all, I wanted to hold this feeling that we had inside me forever. And there in the dark, with Monroe in my arms, I tried to do just that.

• • •

We fell asleep, and when I woke up with blankets tangled around my legs and a warm body cuddled against me, it was her eyes I saw staring up at me. Her eyes and her pink cheeks and that slow smile that got me in the chest every time.

"Hey," I said roughly, kind of choked up as the memories of the night before chased through my mind.

"Hey," she replied softly.

I glanced toward my window. "Guess we're in trouble, huh?"

She nodded. "Yeah. I texted my mother a couple of hours ago and told her we got held up and, uh, were stuck at Brent's without a ride home."

"Shit, really?"

"She was all about coming for me, but I told her that I'd be home for breakfast, and for whatever reason, she let it go."

Monroe exhaled a shaky breath and her lower lip trembled. "What if we don't see each other again? What if you go back to school and fall into your old life and forget all about me? What if all of this slips by as if it never happened and I don't get the chance to be with you again?"

"That's not gonna happen."

A tear slipped down her cheek. "How do you know?"

I leaned my forehead against hers. "Because I promise it won't."

A heartbeat passed between us.

"Nathan?"

"Huh?" I trailed kisses down her neck and it was hard for me to think straight. Hard for me to even hear the words she was saying.

"I love you."

"I know."

"Nathan?"

"Yeah, babe." I was reaching for her mouth. Wanting one more taste.

"Do you think we can do it one more time…you know, since we're in trouble already?"

After that, there was no more talking. After that, there was just the two of us, struggling to stay inside the little cocoon we'd created.

And for now, that was good enough.

# Chapter Thirty-Two
# Monroe

My gram told me once when I was eleven that I could do anything. She'd been very matter of fact as she poured us each an iced tea on a steamy afternoon.

It was the kind of afternoon when the air sizzled and stuck to the insides of your clothes. The kind of afternoon that made your skin clammy and your muscles lazy. I remember that the birds were quiet but the locusts chimed like mini buzz saws.

Funny, the things that you remember, and the things that you can't forget no matter how hard you try.

I think about that now and it seems so long ago.

I've learned a lot since that summer. I've learned that tragedy can strike when you least expect it. That life can disappear.

But I've also learned that life goes on. The world still turns, and every morning, the sun still rises. I learned that while pain and regret can burrow beneath your skin like a parasite, there is always hope.

We just have to be patient and lucky enough to find it. Or if you're like me, it finds you.

Nathan Everets was my hope and I knew that I was his. He was right. Together we could do anything.

It just sucked that our together was going to end in about ten minutes.

"Flight 247, New Orleans to New York, now boarding."

The disembodied voice cut through my thoughts and I squeezed Nate's hands. "That's me."

We stood up and I watched Gram hug Mom and Dad before turning to me. Her silver hair caught a beam of light from the windows, and for a second, I thought she looked like an angel.

An angel who dressed in pearls and linen like a real southern woman.

Nate let go of my fingers and I flew into her arms, fighting the knot of emotion that clogged my throat.

How could I express to my gram everything that I'd felt and experienced this summer? How could I tell her that I think she saved me? That she and Nathan had pretty much kept the crazy out of my head so that I could heal?

"You take care of yourself, you hear?" Gram hugged me fiercely. "I love you so much, my little girl."

"I know."

"Thank you," she said softly, pulling away.

"What for?" I was barely able to get the words out.

"For being strong enough to let me in." She tucked a piece of my hair behind my ear and whispered, for my ears only. "And for catching Nathan."

"Monroe, we've got to board."

I nodded at my mother and watched my dad shake Nathan's hand. The two of them moved off a few paces, and I waited for Nathan to come to me.

"So," he said huskily, "I guess this is it."

I nodded. I couldn't speak because I was too afraid that if I tried to, I would burst into tears and things would get messy real fast.

He gathered me into a hug, his mouth next to my ear. "We'll talk every day."

Again I nodded.

"Skype will be our best friend, right?"

I sniffled. And nodded.

"And when Trevor gets better, I'm bringing him to New York to meet you."

"Okay," I whispered.

"Monroe, we have to go." My mom looked like she was going to cry, and I kissed Nathan, a soft, quick brush of my lips.

"I love you," I said with a smile, my eyes watery and on the verge of leaking like Niagara Falls.

Nate blew out a long breath and gave me one final hug. Then he whispered, "See you soon."

I didn't look back at him as I followed my parents to the

boarding desk. I didn't even look back before heading down the tunnel that took us onto our plane.

I didn't want to remember him standing in the airport lounge with his hands shoved into the pockets of his jeans and his long, sun-kissed hair touching the tops of his shoulders.

That, back there, was good-bye, and good-bye was no longer an option. Not in my world. I grinned. Not in my universe.

Nope. Good-bye didn't exist.

• • •

*A week before Christmas…*

December is a crazy month.

School winds down. Parties seem to take up every weekend. Hanukkah. Christmas. *Birthdays.*

Mine falls on the 20th, which was today, and I was glad my parents had let it go without a big deal. I really hated big deals. Besides, who had time for birthdays when there was still so much to do for the holidays?

It was the Saturday before Christmas, and I'd spent most of it shopping with my best friend, Kate. We'd spent a small fortune on each other—it's so much easier to do when we can pick out our own presents—and I had to search for the perfect gift for Gram.

She was arriving in two days, and I couldn't wait to see her.

"Okay, I have, like, three bags of potato chips, cheese popcorn, and Skor chocolate. What do you want first?" Kate asked.

I tossed a pillow at Kate and made a face. "And you wonder why you've got zits popping up on your chin."

"Junk food has nothing to do with it," Kate grinned. "It's called hormones." She shoved a piece of chocolate in her mouth. "Speaking of hormones, when is Mr. Gorgeous Skyping this week?"

My frown deepened. "He's working late for his uncle on some big project. So maybe later tonight."

"Huh," she said and flopped down beside me. "I have *Love Actually* or *The Notebook*."

I glanced over her shoulder. "Why don't we do both?"

The doorbell went and I yelled, "Mom, the McGills are here."

My parents were going to a Christmas party, so Kate and I had the night ahead of us, and we intended to eat ourselves into a stupor, high on chocolate and popcorn, and watch our favorite movies.

The doorbell went again and I shoved off from the sofa. "Put the movie in, Kate. I'll be right back."

We lived in a large, comfortable brownstone, but our living space went up, not out. This meant that the family/TV room was on the third floor, and by the time I got to the main level, I was breathing a little harder than I'd like.

"Mom," I yelled over my shoulder one more time before opening the door and standing back. It was cold out and snowy. I shivered and then froze. Like really froze. Like my entire body was as still as a deer in the headlights.

I think that maybe my world tilted a little off center. Or the earth moved.

Or maybe my reality had just fallen in on itself and I was in a different dimension. A dimension where my boyfriend—my hot, sweet, amazing boyfriend—was standing on the front stoop with huge, feathery snowflakes glistening in his hair.

"Oh," was all I managed to say.

I didn't want to cry. I didn't want to be that girl who falls apart at the mere sight of the boy she loves.

But holy hell, I was that girl.

The tears started before I could stop them, and then his arms were around me. We were laughing and kissing and crying, and I didn't want to open my eyes because I was so scared that it was all a dream.

"Hey," he said softly, his lips nuzzling my ear.

I wriggled out of his arms. "What are you doing here? Oh my God, Nathan. Why didn't you tell me you were coming?"

I glanced down in horror at my old sweats and the faded, gray T-shirt that used to be white. I had on my bunny slippers, my hair was in a ponytail, and—my hands flew to my chin—there, where I knew he could see the white zit paste.

The white zit paste that was smeared all over his cheek.

"Jesus, Monroe. You weren't kidding. He's hot."

Kate came up behind me, and I heard my parents shuffling behind her. I glanced back and saw that they weren't dressed to go out. In fact, Dad had on his comfy pants, the ones where the zipper was forever falling down.

"Nathan?"

God, I wished we were alone. He looked so handsome in his dark jeans, boots, and heavy jean jacket. His beanie hung off the back of his head, and I loved that there was a bit of stubble on his chin.

My heart squeezed.

"I brought someone to meet you."

He moved aside and I saw a guy standing behind him. He was tall and thin, but his grin was wide and his eyes were so blue they looked like they had the sky in them.

"Trevor?" I asked hesitantly.

He'd come out of his coma a few weeks into September. From what Nathan had said, he had some problems, most of them to do with his memory, but he'd made a slow and steady recovery.

He nodded. "The one and...only. Good...to finally meet you. I've always wanted to come to New York so...I hope you don't mind."

"No, I..." My tongue was so tied up I could barely talk. Oh my God, I sounded like an idiot.

"Okay, this is nice, boys, but I'm not used to this kind of cold. Do you mind moving so an old woman can get to the heat?"

Trevor moved and Gram pushed past, kissing me quickly and touching my cheek as she strode by. Again with the surprises.

I wasn't expecting her for two more days. "Happy birthday, Monroe. You're looking good. Living in the moment suits you."

Nathan grabbed my hand again, and his touch zinged through my entire body. I wasn't just alive. I was on fire. I was where I wanted to be, with the people I wanted to be with.

Life, such as it was, was as perfect as it ever was going to get.

Gram was right.

But then, Gram was always right.

# Acknowledgments

This book, for so many reasons, means a lot to me. I've always wanted to write a young adult novel—one my daughter and her friends could read—and it feels amazing to have done so.

But it took a while, and I need to thank a few people who helped along the way. First off, my writing buddies, Michelle Rowen and Eve Silver. You both were so encouraging and gracious that I'm not sure I could have gone down this road without your prodding! Michelle, you rock the synopsis tweaking, so thank you!

I also need to thank Leah Hultenschmidt for taking the time to read a few chapters and for calling me right away with an offer. Thanks for your thoughts and your drive to make this book the best it could be. Aubrey Poole as well, thanks for grabbing up the reins and helping me get the book all pretty and shiny!

I also am grateful to have found a wonderful agent who I trust implicitly and who has the great taste to be married to a musician! Sara Megibow, you're truly a rock star, and I appreciate all that you do for me.

Thanks also to the many bloggers, readers, and reviewers who've had a hand in getting the word out about my books. Again, so appreciated and I'm humbled daily at the generosity of those in publishing!

Lastly, a big thank-you to my family, my husband Andrew, my kids, Jake and Kristen, and my friends! You guys know and accept the woman who, when under deadline, wears the same sweatpants several days in a row and thinks microwave food is "the best." Thanks for hanging in there with me and seeing my dreams come to fruition!

# About the Author

Juliana Stone fell in love with her first book boyfriend when she was twelve. The boy was Ned, Nancy Drew's boyfriend, and it began a lifelong obsession with books and romance. A tomboy at heart, she split her time between baseball, books, and music—three things that carried over into adulthood. She's thrilled to be writing young adult as well as adult contemporary romance and does so from her home somewhere in Canada.

Don't miss Juliana Stone's
next captivating YA novel...
Coming Summer 2015.

NATHAN AND MONROE FOUND FRIENDSHIP AND
FORGIVENESS—BUT WHAT ABOUT TREVOR?

Trevor Lewis is so far from where he was that he's scared he'll
never find his way back. The accident, the coma—he'll never
be the same. Sometimes, he forgets things, has trouble finding
the right words. It's annoying, frustrating—embarrassing. And
school? Forget it. His parents think a tutor is the answer. Trevor
thinks he's a lost cause. But he'll spend the summer with his
stuck-up new tutor Everly Jenkins, not because he wants to,
but because he has too. Because Everly is his only hope for a
shot at normal.